GALLEON

GALLEON

RUBY SMITH

Matador
9 Priory Business Park,
Wistow Road, Kibworth Beauchamp,
Leicestershire. LE8 0RX
Tel: 0116 279 2299
Email: books@troubador.co.uk
Web: www.troubador.co.uk/matador
Twitter: @matadorbooks

ISBN9781788033374

British Library Cataloguing in Publication Data.
A catalogue record for this book is available from the British Library.

Printed on FSC accredited paper
Printed and bound in Great Britain by 4edge Limited
Typeset in 12pt Bembo by Troubador Publishing Ltd, Leicester, UK

Matador is an imprint of Troubador Publishing Ltd

To Maisie and Edie, because they asked first.

Chapter 1

SCARLET

Her hair was sticking in the blood, catching and pulling on the burns; each strand, drop and ruined piece of skin a grotesquely gorgeous shade of red. She should do something, heal herself, but she just couldn't tear her eyes away from the way her hair fused to the wounds as they wept. That cursed hair, so vibrant, so recognisable and so very, very red. For years she'd lived on Vincent neither harassed nor unnoticed; then something had changed. As she stood there gazing at the blood and burned flesh clinging to those tendrils, Ridley couldn't help but think that the only thing that never changed was her.

She breathed deep, the acrid stench of burning things heavy in the air, feeling the stretch of abused skin with every inhalation. She should heal it all, change the flesh back to its unmarred state. It wouldn't do, this continued notoriety; she'd sworn to remain a Shadow, but the red had to go.

With her damaged hand she clasped her hair as tightly as she could, barely enough sensation left in it to feel the strands as she pulled them from her neck. With her good hand she took up some scissors from the drawer and started to cut, years' worth of hard-won inches sliding through her bloodied fingers as she progressed. She stared at herself in the mirror, ivy eyes gazing at the jagged edges of scarlet that hung high about her neck; it still wouldn't do.

The door behind her opened, and she could see in the reflection Friday's glare, unimpressed storm clouds drinking her in.

"Could the haircut not wait?"

"No." Ridley barely managed to croak out the words, her throat was so damaged by smoke and constricted by blistering skin.

"By the Mother, Ridley, heal yourself, now. Then come out and I'll fix your hair."

She watched Friday leave, tracking that tall, lithe body as it disappeared from sight. Ridley looked down at herself, tracing a ruin with streaming eyes. She took a breath and focused, too used to the feeling of mending flesh to pay it more than fleeting attention. It itched far less than naturally healing skin, but it was warm as it knit itself whole; tingling down into the tips of her now-perfected fingers. When she moved to her neck she gagged, the shifting flesh pulling tight and slack and choking her a little, till that too was whole and unblemished. Ridley took stock of the blood still staining her; all of it her own. It wouldn't take much to replenish what was lost, but she didn't want to. She wanted to savour that shivering, achy tiredness that crept in the wake of fleeting adrenaline; she wanted the sensation to linger.

Friday was waiting for her when she emerged, clad in loose breeches and a vest, all those ginger tresses pulled away from her long neck. Ridley almost smiled. She felt the other woman's eyes, appreciative yet clinical, rake over her.

"Feel better now?"

"I suppose." Ridley sat by Friday's legs, rivulets running in chilled trails down her back. "You?"

Friday hummed her agreement, leaning in close to speak. "Shall I sort your hair?"

"If you don't mind."

They shifted so that Friday was stood behind her, fingers gentle through the clipped feathers.

"And what, pray tell, did your hair do that you felt the need to hack at it in such a fashion?"

Ridley gave no answer, revelling in the cold scrape of scissors against her neck as Friday evened the strands, trusting herself to this fearsome woman's care.

Friday moved round, kneeling before Ridley as though at an altar, face tilted up beseechingly. "Have I not earned the right to know?"

Her hands tightened on Ridley's smaller ones, just enough pressure to make her point.

Ridley relented. "I just don't want it any more. It's like a flame in the dark, and all the moths have sharp teeth." Just above her heart a lightning-bolt mess of a scar splashed out in sharp-angled rivers of brilliant white, one line travelling up over her collarbone and ending just below her left ear. The tip of this Friday traced, raised platinum skin an excruciatingly familiar pattern.

"I'd shield you from them, if you'd let me."

"You'd kill them if I let you."

Friday's brow darkened, rage bubbling over in her typical loss of temper, but the gentle motion of her fingers continued. She spoke, hushed, but deep and steady.

"It's no more than they deserve, the ungrateful little wretches."

"They don't know they've anything to be grateful for."

"Just tell me who they were."

"No."

Ridley watched, silent, as Friday flung herself away. She saw the way anger and frustration vibrated under the other woman's skin, her whole body trembling. Other people could be so casual with Friday, but then they'd never seen what damage she could do; never borne the brunt of it. It was a marvel how she controlled herself when she wanted to; not a single piece of metal in the room rattling or humming with the force of Friday's fury. Even her voice was clipped.

"Why won't you let me defend you?"

"I can defend myself."

"Then why don't you?"

"Because I don't want to."

When Ridley met her eyes she saw a face hardened, all those ugly emotions come out to play on her lover's pretty face. Friday growled.

"Fine. Then it's time to go."

Ridley blinked, watching the resolution settle. "Go?"

"Yes, it's become perfectly apparent that we can't stay on Vincent any longer."

"But you love this house." She wasn't sure why, but

her simple statement deflated Friday, till the woman was once again kneeling before her.

"Do you really think I don't know why you cut your hair?"

Ridley sucked in a breath, the air around them chilled and fresh as the ocean. The kindness was back in those grey eyes, like a patch of blue sky between the clouds. "You'll be a Shadow till the day you die, Ridley, it doesn't mean you have to be happy about it."

Unwelcome words flashed across her mind, images and the feel of lightning through her veins, but she held her tongue. It wouldn't do to anger Friday when she was keen to be kind.

Rather than start another fight she said, "You want to leave the island?"

Friday nodded. "There's no place for us on Vincent any more. The people are growing too used to you to keep their distance."

"To one of the grand continents, then?" Ridley pondered; they were running out of corners to hide away in.

"No, I think it's time we go somewhere they've forgotten us. Where we'll just be a Harlon and her Shadow."

Slowly Ridley's mind came to it: "Gallow."

"Yes."

"No."

"Ridley–"

"Not Gallow, not there. You swore to me–"

"You promised things to me too. When you live as long as we have oaths aren't quite so easy to keep."

Ridley felt the terror blossom in her chest, its claws raking through her veins like a spiteful wild thing. She couldn't go home…

"We won't be, Ridley, we won't go north."

In her fear she must have spoken out loud, but her own voice was like a distant echo in her skull.

"We won't?"

"No. We'll go to the new capital, to Cerrano. Inventors do well there – we can do well there."

"Cerrano, by the lake?"

Friday smiled, so bright and happy her nose crinkled. This close, Ridley could count her freckles, a burnished constellation across a wintry sky.

"That's right, by the lake. The town we helped build; imagine what it must be like now."

Gradually Ridley acquiesced, calming till her heart slowed and that terror receded to a dull ache. Friday went back to her hair, agile fingers combing through the scarlet strands. Suddenly she took a fistful, tugging Ridley's head back so her neck arched, just the right side of painful. Those granite eyes bore down on her.

"Tell me you love me, Ridley."

"I love you, Friday."

With a contended smile she let go, resuming her work.

Ridley whispered, "Do you believe me?"

"Always."

Chapter 2

GOLD

They all had high hopes for the new girl from Bound. Lara could practically feel it, all that expectation clogging up her pores and settling heavy on her skin. Near the front she could see the last new girl, Commander King; Jackie. Stood tall in all her finely-honed glory, same iridescent platinum-and-silver features as Lara's, but carved by the years into stalwart perfection. She pondered: what would they make of her after such a creature; who was Lara Key compared with the mighty Jackie King?

Someone bumped into her, as all around fellow cadets jostled and strove to see their new leaders onstage. Deceptively lithe muscles kept Lara static as the others swarmed, bouncing off her in muted surprise. She was the only one Bound had sent this year, and she felt it, stood alone amongst the other cadets, like a bright, lonely boat on a stormy sea. Lara looked at Jackie again; at least the lighthouse wasn't far away.

So focused was she that when Lara finally pulled her gaze away she realised the noise had died down, and up on the stage stood the imposing High Commissioner Stone. Tall, sturdy, a little ashen, Stone looked like the Highfort itself. Lara pushed her shoulders back, instinctively standing to attention, but her eyes drifted. Jackie was motionless, perfectly attentive to her leader as though every word spoken was pure perfection. However, it seemed the commander was aware of more than just the commissioner. Slowly those silver eyes turned to Lara's, one blonde brow perfectly arched as if to say, *Shouldn't you be paying attention?* Lara snapped back to the stage, feeling the heat crawl up her neck; she only prayed Jackie couldn't see how red she must have been from up there. Chancing a surreptitious glance back, she had worried for naught. Jackie was back at attention; a twinge of disappointment ran through her.

Finally Lara paid heed to the commissioner, that all-powerful voice compelling her to do her duty.

"Many of you, I am sure, have dreamt of this moment. The Cerranites amongst you most of all. But know this: the life of a Greycoat is not for the faint of heart. You must work, you must be vigilant, dedicated, and strive to uphold all we hold dear. Your life is now in the service of this great city and your fellows in arms. Times change, but the Greycoats remain steadfast, and Cerrano continues to prosper. Though you be but cadets, you must act as we act, and stay true. *Serve only the righteous.*"

As the Greycoat motto rang out across the courtyard, Lara watched the others preen, anticipation a current jumping from one to the next, but her chest was empty.

She thought it funny that after all the years of being chastised for being so easily excitable, she should be the sedate one now. Perhaps her trainers really did beat it out of her. Suddenly the cadets parted, and she was face-to-face with Jackie King.

"You must be Cadet Key." Her voice was that clipped, regimental tone the Bound-born always wielded; all except for Lara. She recalled being scolded for it before, letting joy and fear show in the frenetic cadence of her voice. She wouldn't make that mistake again.

"Commander King."

"Our people do well here, Key, you're the only one to prove that this year. Don't let us down."

Lara nodded. "No, ma'am. I won't."

Another figure appeared to Jackie's left, uniform a touch more adorned yet worn a little less formally. She had soft-looking skin, painted all over in warm shades of gold from her head to her fingertips. Something pleasing tingled beneath Lara's breast at the sight, the light of this woman so much warmer and less blinding than Jackie's; so much more inspiring. The commander turned, and Lara watched her face soften to something almost sweet.

"Deputy Commissioner." Even her voice had lost its edges, the newcomer's title emerging as a hushed prayer from scarred lips.

The deputy commissioner came closer, eyes glowing like the rest of her, and gave them both a subtle smile.

"Commander King." Lara's breath caught as that attention shifted to her, the woman speaking softly. "And you must be Lara Key?"

"Y-yes, ma'am."

"My name is Roman Ion."

"Deputy Commissioner Ion."

"Yes, I'm well aware of my title, thank you, Jackie." The laughter in Roman's voice caught Lara off guard, as did Jackie's contented hum in response. Somehow the deputy commissioner must have sensed her panic, because in the next moment she was leaning in conspiratorially, whispering, "I've been told informality is unbecoming in one of my rank. But I can't seem to help myself."

"I suppose it doesn't help instil command."

Lara clamped her mouth shut, horrified at her own outburst. She glanced to Jackie, who merely raised that platinum brow once again. Yet Roman, when she looked back, looked pleased.

"True." She leant in again, this time close enough for Lara to smell her, peaches and heat and a myriad of rich, summery things. "But I find it instils something better."

From across the courtyard someone called for Roman, and reluctantly Lara felt her move away. Before she went, she addressed Jackie.

"The commissioner and I are leaving for Sevo's funeral; you're in charge whilst we're gone."

Jackie nodded, watching Roman go with a slightly more controlled expression than that which Lara was sure adorned her own face.

"Loyalty."

Lara jumped, so focused on that fading figure that she hadn't felt the commander move beside her.

"Pardon, ma'am?"

"If you're wondering what the better thing Roman's infectious informality instils, it's loyalty."

Chapter 3

ASH

It was raining, of course it was; Ash would have laughed to see it. Not that he'd ever laugh again, or smile or yell or, well, do anything. Ash Marty Sevo was dead, and Watt still hadn't managed to say it out loud. It played on a loop in his mind, over and over till everything else was just background noise and the words melded to form a hideous din. Watt was alive, Ash was dead, and it was raining as they buried him.

He turned to Modesto, perpetual scowl softened by their situation; even his hair looked a duller shade of red. Black suited his old friend ill, made him drawn and pale, but that couldn't all be blamed on the colour, he supposed. The circumstances must take some responsibility. One of Modesto's scraped hands was clutching the stem of his umbrella so tightly Watt swore he could hear it creaking over the steady pitter-patter of rain. He followed the trail of the man's other arm to where his hand rested, gentle as could be, upon Wes' small shoulder.

Wes Sevo, only thirteen, watching his father be buried in trembling silence. Modesto had never had children, and Watt's own daughter stood to his right was long grown; yet it was to them this lonely boy had been entrusted. Watt watched those frail shoulders shake, tight black curls dampened to sorrow by the rain, and felt the old engine of his heart stutter. The four of them would have to learn themselves anew, discover what they were without Ash at the centre of their world. Watt couldn't help but think what a bleak world it was.

All too soon he heard the thud as Ash's coffin touched the earth, and the litany in his head finally began to slow. He glanced back at the boy, stock-still; the finality of wood meeting dirt painful enough to halt even a child's tremors. Wes was meant to move forward, to use one of his small hands to throw the first handful of dirt onto his father's coffin; yet he remained frozen. Watt caught Modesto's eye, those bottle-green pools desperate and a little unsure; it suited him worse than the black. Watt nodded, and with a gentle squeeze of Wes' shoulder, Modesto moved forward.

He watched the staunch set of his friend's shoulders; still white-knuckling the umbrella as he slowly bent and grasped a handful of sodden dirt. As Modesto stood Watt felt a hand grip his, but when he looked Wes was still staring straight ahead.

"Do you want me to go up with you?" He spoke quietly, scared that even with the continual drumming of rain his voice might shatter the scene. Rather than answer,

Wes slowly moved forward, hand still tight around the older man's. Together they moved, and as if sensing them, Modesto moved to the side. Wordlessly Watt handed his own umbrella to his friend and knelt to gather a fistful of dirt. It was wet and sticky in his hand, the clumps cold against his skin. The strong smell of earth invaded his nostrils, and in his own melancholy moment he thought that maybe the rain was Ash's tears, letting them know just how sad he was to leave them all behind.

The chorus in his head picked up again – *Ash Marty Sevo is dead* – and then he brought the dirt to his lips and whispered, "Till the next life, old friend." Reluctantly he let it go, watching helplessly as the clumps fell onto the shining teak coffin where his friend now lay.

He felt Evie come up beside him as Watt looked to Wes again. The rain slid down the back of his collar as his daughter clutched his elbow; it wouldn't do to cry yet. With his little fist at his lips Wes spoke, quietly but painfully loud to Watt's ears.

"Till the next life, Daddy." Then he let go, the four of them watching the dirt as it hit, and the words ran through Watt's mind one last time: *Ash Marty Sevo is dead.*

Perhaps the silence was worse – it certainly seemed so, the steady pounding of rain no replacement now the cacophony in Watt's brain had quieted. It was a shivering, stinging attempt at comfort, the way the rain trickled in the small spaces to get beneath his clothes; running between his and Wes' still-joined hands. A warm, calloused hand on the back of his neck brought him round, and as Modesto handed him back his umbrella Watt welcomed his friend's perpetual warmth.

He leant in and spoke softly. "I suppose it's time to thank people for coming."

Modesto grunted. "I don't see why. We didn't ask them to."

"Mods."

"I'm not in the mood for fucking niceties in the rain."

"When has anyone ever expected niceties from you?"

The other man nearly smiled, just a small, weak upturn at the corner of his mouth; yet Watt felt it like a fire in his chest.

Wes tugged at both of their hands, "Should we go speak to the soldiers?"

Watt glanced at them all, an unsure sea of red and silver that'd watched their beloved leader's final performance. He caught Evie's eye as she replied.

"That's all right; Leon and I are taking charge for today." He smiled gratefully at her, accepting his daughter's embrace with desperate affection. "I'll see you all back at the house; don't talk to anyone you don't want to, you don't owe them anything."

As grateful as he was for her kind words and even kinder embrace, Watt sighed as she left, glancing at the sea of black still milling around.

"The commissioner's here, we best see her first."

Modesto's voice stopped him. "What about Shine? I'm fairly certain I saw her lurking about."

"*Governor Shine* will no doubt be with Commissioner Stone, now come along. It wouldn't do for us to ignore them."

If he'd been in the mood Watt was sure he'd have laughed to have Wes so acquiescent whilst Modesto sulked behind them. As it was he simply held his head high, and led their little train to greet the mourners. He caught sight of Shine first, black suit pressed finely and sheltered under her assistant's umbrella. She straightened at their approach, the same practised look on her face as always. Modesto hung back, and Watt took his mantle.

"Governor Shine, thank you for coming."

"Of course, the Steam Syndicate is very important to Cerrano, and Sevo was as beloved as they come. He will most assuredly be missed."

"Thank you, Governor, that means a lot. *Doesn't it, Modesto?*"

"Quite assuredly."

The governor cleared her throat. "Yes. Well, my condolences – I am sure the goddess Fortella has taken him safely to the next life. Watterson, Modesto, Wes." She nodded at each in turn, the last to Wes a little slower before leaving, entourage close at her heels. Watt rounded on his friend.

"As always, Modesto, thank you for your stellar input."

"You know I can't stand that woman, addressing us as though we're friends or–"

"You can't stand anyone. How many times... no. Not today." Watt took a deep breath, his annoyance only calmed by the apology gleaming in his friend's eyes. "You deal with Stone, all right? Keep your temper."

"Yes, all right."

"Roman's here!"

Wes' happy exclamation startled them both, and as he looked up Watt saw the two Greycoats deep in conversation. Wes tugged on his hand; despite their morning so far Watt found himself pleased to see them. As they made their way over he realised Roman and Stone looked to be one step away from an argument, the former particularly close to bursting. They were so embroiled Watt managed to catch the end of their conversation before they noticed him.

"… Just don't think it's appropriate, or particularly kind."

"Kind? Far be it from me to intentionally upset them, Roman, but the governor wants it done today."

"Wants what done?"

They both appeared unmoved by Modesto's growl, though Watt could see the unease on Roman's face.

"Teach, Cinnabar, my condolences. And to you, Sevo, most of all. May Fortella escort your father swiftly to Io Sola."

Wes grimaced, befuddlement clear on his face as he turned to Watt. He cleared his throat.

"Thank you, Commissioner Stone, it means a lot."

"All manners aside, Shine wants what done?"

They looked to Modesto, whose cold gaze was locked on the commissioner.

"Ah yes, that." Stone straightened, and Watt couldn't tamp down his feelings of dread when he saw the resigned look on Roman's face. "Since the tragedy, the Citadel believes it time stricter measures were put in place to ensure people's safety."

Watt balked. "Stricter measures?" Before the commissioner could respond, a voice from another group called her away.

"My apologies, gentlemen, it seems I'm needed. But I leave Deputy Commissioner Ion to relay all necessary information."

With that she gave Roman a hearty slap on the back and left, her second in command watching her go, aghast.

"So, *Deputy Commissioner Ion*, care to elaborate?" Modesto's tone was mocking, but Watt could see the tension in his friend's frame; as if today hadn't been trying enough. He watched as Roman looked at Wes, her golden glow dampened but not diminished. When she spoke it was measured, to soothe his friend's temper.

"The Citadel feel, in the light of what happened, that it is time measures are put in place to ensure the future safety of Steam Syndicate members."

"And what," Modesto was spitting through his teeth, still well aware of where they were and who they were with, "measures would these be?"

"I'm very sorry about Ash. He was a good man."

"Yes he was, Roman, now tell us what fucking measures the Citadel have deigned to inflict on us."

"The Citadel will send an envoy to oversee the syndicate for a period of time, in which they will assess the environment in which you work."

Watt stopped his friend before he started, a placating hand held out.

"And should they find us unsatisfactory?"

"You will be required to make changes."

Watt weighed his words, looking from Wes' downcast face to Modesto's stuttering fury before replying.

"And if we should refuse to make these changes?"

A few seconds passed in which only the rain and

distant chatter of people echoed around. He looked back to Roman. Her voice was soft and kind, but it could not undo the finality of her words.

"Then you will be shut down."

Chapter 4

RISE

In Bound your fellow soldiers were your life, be they kind or cruel; so Lara hadn't been overly concerned with who her cadet partner would be. Hadren Gogh, as it turned out, didn't appear to be either of those things, but Lara wasn't entirely sure what she was as opposed to what she wasn't. She glanced at her across the table, the other woman gulping down massive bites of her breakfast. She'd a golden hoop through her left nostril and another in her right eyebrow, which stood out so glaringly against the sable of her skin that Lara couldn't help her eyes drifting back to them.

"My parents are Ajartan."

Lara blinked, suddenly finding Hadren's eyes locked with her own.

"Pardon?"

"You keep looking, thought I'd sate your curiosity. In Ajarta, we pierce."

"Why?" Lara twirled her spoon in her hand; she really needed to get her mouth under control.

Hadren shrugged. "I'm not sure. Mamarra's often depicted with adornments, so I suppose it must be something to do with her."

"As gods go she is one of the more elaborate ones."

Hadren smirked, spooning another large bite before continuing. "Why d'you want to know anyway? No Ajartans in Bound?"

Lara fidgeted, hitting her spoon painfully against her fingers.

"Where you're born doesn't really matter. When you're from Bound, you're from Bound. We had Ajartans, Xinthans, Tegarrats – except we didn't really."

Hadren inclined her head, chewing long and slow in what Lara assumed must be deep thought. But then, glancing at her food, she figured the other woman could just be deciphering some mystery taste.

She spoke once she'd finally swallowed. "So you've never seen piercings before?"

"I'd never left Bound before."

Hadren's face made an abortive movement, as if her jaw wanted to drop but she wouldn't allow it.

Lara went on, "I was just surprised the Greycoats allowed you to keep them."

"Why wouldn't they?"

"It's just…" she hunted for the right word, watching that golden hoop climb as Hadren's eyebrow quirked, "unique."

"Unique?"

"Noticeable, I mean, maybe. Uhm…"

"Personal?"

A reminder, she thought, of what you were, who you were before Bound. Lara didn't think she had a before; she certainly wasn't allowed one.

"Yes, personal. Does Commissioner Stone not mind?"

"I don't think she really notices. Deputy Commissioner Ion though, she does."

Lara smiled, thinking of gold and warmth; of Roman.

Hadren laughed. "From that dozy smile I figure you've met her."

"Yesterday, at the ceremony. So, Rom… Deputy Commissioner Ion doesn't mind?"

"No. Roman doesn't mind."

Once breakfast was over they were given their assignments, Hadren leading the way. Lara followed eagerly, excitement thrumming though her marrow.

"So, you're sure you know the way?"

Hadren feigned offence. "Know the way? I'll have you know I was born and bred here. Not an inch of Cerrano I don't know."

"That must have been exciting, I didn't get to see much of it on the way in."

Hadren halted abruptly, throwing Lara a look she couldn't decipher.

"Lara Key, are you telling me you got off an airship, went to the Highfort and stayed there?"

"Yes."

"When did you arrive?"

"Three days ago."

Hadren spluttered. "Wha… why didn't you go out?"

Lara thought back to Bound, to the trainers and the officers, to the cadence of her own voice and the emotions they always accused her of wearing so openly. *When you wear your heart on your sleeve it's easy to take, Key. They'll take it, tread on it, pull it apart. Because that's what it means to the world, Key, that's what an ineffective soldier means: nothing.*

"Because no one said I could." She wasn't sure what Hadren was seeing, but whatever it was it was enough for her gaze to change.

"Why don't we take the long way?"

Hadren took her through the Static Forest, the frozen metal heart of Cerrano, where the noise of the city bounced off the solid tree trunks and ricocheted round.

"How'd they get like this?"

"A wizard came, back when Cerrano was a little village by a lake. Or so they say, anyway." She took Lara through the hustle of Market Town, marvelling at the colours and splendour and the smells permeating the late winter wind. They went through the Outlands, where the narrow, winding streets opened up into boulevards lined by bare trees and grand houses.

"Hadren, don't we need to get to the Rise?"

"We are, this is just the scenic route."

Lara smiled, the warmth in her chest burning like an inferno.

Eventually they made it to their destination. Lara wasn't sure what she'd been expecting, but her imagination didn't compare to the real thing. The Rise, sat up on a hill overlooking the rest of Cerrano, was where the temples sat. All the many gods of Eera, the first of the Mother's

Children, built high up above the smoke and noise of the city.

Hadren gestured. “Which temples did Commander King ask us to patrol? Likke?”

“Lyra, Vrya, Whytha and Diana.”

“That’s right. The quiet ones, should be an easy morning.”

“I thought this was your first patrol too?”

“It is, but I live here; I know where people go.”

Together they worked through the crowds, hordes of people buffering Lara against the biting hilltop breeze. They wandered by a great open plaza, past a momentous, partially frozen reflecting pool, and headed into a set of labyrinthine alleys till they came out into another, smaller open space.

“Hadren, what are these spaces for?”

“Hmm? Oh, this is the West Plaza, there are four of them. People hold rallies, mass prayers; whatever takes their fancy.”

“I see.” She didn’t; Lara looked at the people gathering, chaos clambering to have a say, and felt her brain spark. She’d no doubt she was more than capable of dispersing them, but she couldn’t for the life of her figure out what could be so important that they’d want the whole city to hear it.

“You a Gallara worshipper, then?”

“Pardon?”

Lara looked back to Hadren, who was staring at her in that unfathomable way again.

“Sorry, I shouldn’t assume. It’s just Bound is the seat of the army, so I thought warfare would be what your lot looked to.”

"The officers prayed a lot, but we weren't really given the opportunity. Our superiors were basically our gods – why do you keep looking at me like that?"

Hadren's brow was twitching, her voice high-pitched. "What do you expect when you keep saying things like that?"

"Like what?"

Hadren threw her hands up, a desperate sound issuing from her mouth. "Never mind."

A loud cheer erupted throughout the plaza, both of them looking on as the crowd surged to the raised platform.

Hadren sighed. "What in Io Sola are the liberationists doing here this early?"

Up on the stage, two women began speaking, people cheering as their voices carried. Lara moved towards her partner.

"Who are they?"

"Liberationists." At Lara's nonplussed look, she continued. "Non-magical folk trying to improve their lot."

"What's wrong with their lot?"

Hadren gave her that look again, and Lara felt as though she were missing something.

"Considering they can't join the Greycoats, hold office in the Citadel or have any real say in their lives, not much. And that's just in Cerrano. What happened to the non-magical ones in Bound?"

"They were sent away or…"

"Or?"

"If they were strong enough physically they were trained as foot soldiers for the army."

"Right."

Lara gazed back at the stage as the two women continued. She couldn't quite hear them but their listeners appeared enthralled. Hadren's hand on her arm stole her attention.

"Come on, there are other officers patrolling the plazas; we've a job to do. And as much as I respect their cause, no good ever came from listening to those two." She gestured disparagingly at the women onstage, Lara glancing back till they'd walked out of sight.

"Who are they?"

"Evie Teach and Shoshanna something-or-other. I've known Evie for years, she'd always been a touch overdramatic, especially since..." She stopped abruptly, looking almost apologetic. "It doesn't matter."

"You agree with them, then?"

Hadren looked Lara over; she'd never felt so exotic before.

"I agree with what they stand for."

Her mind whirled, but she swallowed her opinion, recanting the words ingrained in her for years.

"Surely they're where they are for a reason – if things weren't the best they could be they'd have been changed by now."

"Do you really believe that, Lara?" Hadren's hazel eyes were earnest, and Lara thought back to the casual way she'd said Roman's name, to their shared Cerranite charm; to the way they said *her* name like it meant something. Maybe her mind would be all right.

"No."

Hadren smiled. "Why not?"

"Because in Bound there's no difference between a foot soldier and cannon fodder."

Chapter 5

MODESTO

Modesto was brilliant, Watt had known it from the moment they'd met. He was a genius, dreaming up engines and machines and sketching a future where people without magic didn't feel inferior. Hope was what Modesto gave Watt, hope for them all, but of course not everyone could see it. It was the younger man's demeanour, he supposed; his friend had never been any good at explaining, he hadn't the time for it. Yet even with all this in mind Watt still found himself surprised, come the morning of their return to work, to be greeted by an irate Leon Tsaika barely an hour into the day.

"Wait, wait; he's done what?"

"He's crawled into the new engine and is refusing to come out till it works. My pointing out to him the dangers of the situation didn't seem to change his plans."

Watt took a deep breath, the smells of oil, sweat and dust thick in the air; it was a small comfort. Leon's dark eyes, however, were doing their best to do away with that comfort. She was a sharp-featured person, not long arrived from Orysan in the very far south of Eera, her words still curling syllables like smoke. Ash had liked her, and she'd risen through the ranks quickly, but none of that mattered to Modesto.

"I'm sure he didn't mean–"

She snorted. "I can assure you he did. It doesn't matter, not even he can get that thing working any time soon, but he's still asking for an accident doing what he's doing."

She slipped into the seat opposite, red uniform stripped down to its working state; sleeves rolled up and collar loose. It should have been an easy day.

"He's clearly under a lot of stress, Watt, but so are you. And yet here you sit, not climbing into machinery while yelling at everyone to mind their *own fucking business.*"

Watt choked. "Leon, you know Modesto well enough by now. He just doesn't know how to deal with his grief." She nodded but didn't look mollified, so he continued. "You've been invaluable through all of this, dealing with the others and overseeing reconstruction. By Garrin, dealing with Modesto and myself. Don't let his bad temper get to you. I'll speak with him."

His sincerity must have shone through, because in the next moment she sent him a smile.

"Fine."

Watt sighed in relief; however Leon wasn't quite finished.

"But don't let this wait, Watt, it'll only get worse."

With a last salute she left, and Watt watched her go in weariness. He'd speak with Modesto, he would, but not yet.

With a groan he laid his head atop his folded arms, desk creaking with the weight. By the Mother, he was tired, his duties as the more professional one all the harder without Ash as a go-between; he couldn't temper his remaining partner alone. Although, he mused, perhaps dealing with Modesto's fits of grief would save him from his own.

A soft knock on his door echoed through the room, and craning his head up, he was greeted by Wes.

"Were you sleeping?"

He chuckled. "No, Wes, just resting my tired mind. How can I help you?" He sat up fully, wincing as his back creaked in protest.

"I wanted to look at some of your plans."

"Mine?" The sheepish look on the boy's face told him all he needed to know. "Ah, you want to see some of Mods' designs. What on Eera for?"

Wes shrugged, coming up to Watt smelling of cinnamon and grease.

"I want to make some of my own."

"A fine thing, but perhaps start with some of mine or… or Ash's. Mods' aren't for the unexperienced."

"One of yours and one of Dad's, then?"

"As you wish."

From his innermost pocket he pulled out a small set of keys, leaving the gold and removing the silver.

"Can I open it?"

Watt scowled. "Absolutely not, you know how dangerous the vault is."

"Mods let me."

"He wh… he did not." He turned, smirking down at the boy and pointing. "Don't you try that with me, Wes Sevo."

Wes looked at him with wide eyes, the picture of innocence; Watt's daughter used to use that technique. "And you can put those away too – I'll open the vault and then you and I can look together."

"Should we ask the lady if she wants to see the vault?"

He frowned. "What lady?"

Before any more could be said a resounding crash rattled about the building. Watt's heart froze.

"This guy better be a damned genius, Ash."

"Oh, for the Mother's sake, it's just Bell Town, Watt; it's not like I marched you all the way to Berra."

Watt scoffed, glaring at Ash's ridiculous smile, those damned sharp teeth of his on full display. "Besides, I thought you could do with the exercise."

"Hey!" Ash's arm curled around his neck swiftly, and Watt did his best to ignore that infallibly irritating charm.

"Look, we've known each other forever, and I love you so much it's stupid. But you sitting hunched over those designs all day and night isn't doing you any favours. They'll stop flocking to your bed before you know it."

Before he could rebuke his friend's not-quite-unfounded claims they came to a halt, the small, haphazard garage clanging noisily before them.

"Is this it?" Ash let out a gasp, long arm pulling Watt in closer. "Is this it? My good Watterson, this is the establishment of one Modesto Cinnabar, a Garrin-blessed prodigy if ever there was one!"

"What kind of a name is Modesto Cinnabar?"

"Harlon, I think."

"What? You didn't say he was a Harlon."

"Now, Watt, what kind of backwards attitude is that?"

Watt sighed, shrugging off Ash's arm and reluctantly shuffling inside.

"That's more like it!"

The clanging grew louder, and heat and motion greeted them enthusiastically as they stepped through the door. A gear-shaped blur came sailing through the air towards them, Watt squawking as he ducked.

"Fucking Io Sola, this is what happens when you come to Bell Town. Chaos – chaos and flying things."

Ash's laugh boomed around the workshop, evidently startling whoever was amidst the wreckage and parts as a pained yell erupted from somewhere amongst it all. Watt winced; the resounding clang that preceded it rattled down his bones.

"You all right in there?" Ash hurried forward, peering worriedly at someone, or something. "Sorry, didn't mean to scare you."

A head popped up, dark ginger hair dotted with oil and grease and what, very possibly, looked like blood. It mumbled something which made Ash smile, worry bleeding off his face as he helped the person out of the wreckage. As Watt moved closer the person turned, and he was greeted by the glaring green eyes of a disgruntled boy.

"Watterson Teach, allow me to introduce…"

"Modesto." Without a second thought he was out the door, plummeting down the iron stairs to the workshop floor. His pulse thrummed, all noise and notice zeroed in on the voices below. He felt sick, images of smoke and dirt and… and then he saw Modesto. Stood amongst a pile of broken parts, clutching his forehead whilst two apprentices fussed around him. Watt's breath slowed, and his heart beat settled.

Ignoring everything else he came forward, stopping practically on top of his friend and whispering, "You all right?"

"As ever."

Watt leant in, scrutinising the steady stream of blood trickling from above Modesto's eyebrow.

Modesto grunted. "I'm flattered, Watt, but this is hardly the time."

"Keep still, you moron – hand me that, would you?" He gestured to a nearby worker, who gratefully passed him the clean cloth and bandages they'd fetched. "Come sit down."

"I don't need to sit down, I need to fix this." At that Modesto gave a fallen piece of debris a gentle nudge, scowling down at it.

Watt grabbed his arm, pulling him over to a nearby bench. When he looked back he saw everyone watching: apprentices, security; even Wes was stood at the bottom of the stairs staring.

"Bloody, stupid thing was too heavy for its stand."

"I don't care, and neither do they. Look." He gestured about the room to where their workers were staring unabashed. "You're worrying everyone, not to mention me and Wes. So sit still and let me fix your stupid head."

He couldn't tell if guilt or embarrassment stayed his friend, but whatever it was it was enough for him to sit placidly through Watt's barrage of protective abuse.

"Could you not leave off on this stuff for one day? You aggravate everyone into leaving you to it–"

"Ow."

"Sorry." Watt dabbed at Modesto's forehead a little softer, wiping away the blood till it was clean enough for him to really see the wound. "It's not so bad. Lucky you have such a thick head."

Just then Wes appeared holding a jar of ointment, looking on Modesto in very much the way Ash always had.

"Are you all right, Mods?"

"He's fine, Wes, this is just what we need. Thank you."

Modesto scowled at Watt's interruption, expression darkening as his old friend took the jar from Wes and opened it.

"That's not coming anywhere near me."

"It'll stop the bleeding."

"I don't care, it stings."

Watt was aghast. "I'd imagine dropping an engine on your head hurts no less."

"It barely clipped me."

"Oh right, well, that's fine then." In an instant he'd a hold of his friend, strong arms tight around the other's chest. "Wes, you do the honours."

The young boy cackled, taking a decent amount of the salve and applying it liberally over Modesto's forehead as he struggled.

"Ah! This is mutiny!"

Wes paused, tilting his head. "But you're not a captain."

"Quite right, Wes, his ship fell on him."

Someone to the side coughed, the three of them freezing and looking across to where Leon stood with another woman. She was tall, young and clad in the cream and purple colours Watt would recognise anywhere. He slowly pulled away from Wes and Modesto, standing and smiling as warmly as he was able.

"Ah, hello. Leon, who would this be?"

Leon, to her credit, was desperately trying to remain placid, although he was struggling to tell whether she wanted to laugh or cry.

Clearing her throat, she spoke. "This is Andromeda Knight. The envoy from the *Citadel*."

"Pleased to meet you; you've come to inspect our–"

"Safety."

Watt looked back to Modesto, smeared trails of blood still on his head, then to the broken parts scattered all over the floor, and then back to Andromeda, whose indigo eyes were tracking him like a hawk.

"Forgive me, but did you just say a ship fell on Modesto Cinnabar?"

Chapter 6

TEMPORALITY

The last time they'd seen Cerrano, all those hundreds of years ago, it'd been nothing much at all. Just a tiny village on the shores of Dolce Lake, a great forest to the south but little else besides. Friday hadn't seen much in it. Yet on the horizon to the north, across the lake and green fields, Ridley had seen the silhouette of the Queens Peak; the tallest mountain on Gallow. Sat below that mountain, ensconced on all sides by the spine range and a lake of its own, was Berra, the capital; the seat of royalty. She couldn't help but wonder what the Pentagalents would think to see another place sharing their plateau, sharing the heart of Gallow with them. She'd admit to herself that she'd been in a crueller place back then, eager to cause trouble but unwilling to deal with the consequences. So she and Friday had put the wheels in motion, set Cerrano on its course and promptly left. She wasn't entirely sure what they'd be returning to, believing the stories to be hyperbole at best, but Ridley had been wrong before.

"By Bayona, look at it." Friday's smile leaked into her voice, as she practically skipped from the airship to cast her gaze over the city below.

Ridley followed silently, the smells of fires, food and oh so many people crowding in. No gulls, no sea breeze; the abundance of humanity was, for the first time in a long time, refreshing.

Friday grabbed her hand as they walked over the swiftly diminishing snow, mingling easily with the throngs of people. "Look at our little village now. Look what they've done, Ridley."

Friday's unbridled joy was infectious, and Ridley was only too happy to let a grin take over her face. She felt warm, the low winter sun soaking into her pale skin, and, as she looked at Friday, she was young again. Her lover's joy eclipsed everything else, tightening her grip she pulled Friday in, wrapping her free arm around her neck and pouring every ounce of happiness and passion into a kiss that'd been a long time coming. As they broke apart Friday caught Ridley's bottom lip gently between her teeth, giving it a gentle bite before pulling back just enough to let go. Their breath mingled as they panted, and Ridley felt Friday's body humming with excitement.

Her voice was fond as she spoke. "There's my girl."

Reluctantly they pulled apart, hands still entwined as they picked up their bags and made their way into the city. Ridley took stock of all the people, all the colours of them; Cerrano was the heart of a new world after all.

"Do you remember the way to the tower?" Friday was squinting into the distance. "It's by Dolce, isn't it?"

"Yes." Ridley answered distractedly, eyes trained on a gargantuan bastion sat to the east; towers and garrets looming. "What's that?" They stopped, Friday huffing in disgust.

"I suppose it's the Citadel."

"Citadel?"

"Mm. If I remember correctly the government sits on the southern side, and the rest of it belongs to the Greycoats. You know the police I mentioned? Their side has a different name, but I've quite forgotten it."

"The Greycoats."

Friday made a disgruntled sound of acquiescence. "That's what I said. Now let's go, I'm getting hungry." She pulled Ridley away, but the Shadow kept casting a glance back. The northern side was taller and darker and infinitely more menacing; it seemed the Greycoats didn't want anyone forgetting where they were.

Working their way north, they eventually came upon a colourful sea of market stalls, full of people selling and yelling and getting on with their day. They stopped at a stall filled with fruit, gleaming hues crying out from their chaotically stacked perches.

Friday leant in to her. "Hungry, girl?"

"I wouldn't say no."

"You never do." The other smirked as she turned to the vendor, a man greying and balding all at once.

When Ridley looked up she found he was staring at her, eyes wide; though it was surprise she noted on his face rather than fear.

Friday growled, "Two of those apples, *if you don't mind*."

The poor man blinked, stuttering out an apology as he gathered their request. Ridley smiled, pressing her front against Friday's side and nuzzling her jawline. She could feel the warmth of the other woman leeching in, sliding the fingers of her right hand between the buttons of Friday's shirt.

"Friday, do be nice."

"Don't you flirt with me, Ridley Ripley. Not when I'm not sure if there's a bed waiting for us at the damn clock tower."

Ridley pushed onto her tiptoes, mouth brushing against Friday's ear. "Who needs a bed?"

The tower was very much how she remembered it when they arrived, clock face still a shining hue of pearl, deep silver numbers and an array of intricate rose-gold carvings. It wasn't quite as grand as it had once been, other buildings growing just tall enough to lessen its impact without obscuring that delicate face. Ridley looked at it now, stone walls a little worse for wear, but nothing she couldn't easily fix.

"Did I ever tell you how much I like this tower?"

She looked back at Friday, who was smiling at her in a way that made her whole body shiver.

"Actually, you told me it was ostentatious."

Friday hummed, stalking closer. "That doesn't sound like me."

"Perhaps not now." Ridley smirked as Friday wound her arms around her, a thin, long-fingered hand finding its way beneath her shirt onto the small of her back. A warm point on her chilled skin. "You were going through a despotic phase if I recall correctly."

"Oh, that's right. And you never forget."

"No, Friday, I never forget."

Ridley pulled away, heart bereft as that warm hand fell away, only the remnants of tingling heat slowly bleeding from her back. She approached the door, brushing away years' worth of dust and grime to clear out the keyhole. Then she opened up her jacket and pulled out a hefty set of keys, as behind her Friday groaned, "By the gods, you and your bloody keys."

"How else are we meant to get in?"

"Ridley, that key is centuries old. Do you really think–"

The sound of scraping metal silenced her, the mechanism crunching and grinding out dirt and rust as Ridley fought to turn the key.

"Well, all right then."

Ridley chuckled, but her mirth was short-lived as the door, though unlocked, refused to budge. Leaning on it, feeling the grain snag her clothing and paint flecks fall away, she gave all she could. She heard Friday snort and turned to glare.

"All right, *Bayona*, let's see you get it open."

"Now, now, physical strength was never your forte, my dear Shadow." With a haughty smile the Harlon shouldered the door, a small squeak underlying the loud crack that echoed as she collided painfully with the wood.

"My, what a mighty display of strength."

"You hush your mouth, girl." Pulling back, Friday

scowled at the wood, tracing the stone archway with her eyes. "You'll need to get it open."

"Me?"

"Yes, you, it's all wood and stone, which I won't take offence to this once. Especially when metal could have done the job just as well..."

"I don't mess with wood."

"You did last time we were here."

"Exactly. And I don't intend to repeat that particular mistake."

Friday threw up her hands, letting out a small whine. "*By the gods*, you irritate me."

She shrugged. "And yet you love me."

"That I do." Friday flung herself into the door. "Shall I count the ways, dearest Shadow?" Another bang rattled the air. "How about a song?" And another. "Or perhaps a sonnet of some sort?" Still the door held fast, heedless of Friday's attempts at bludgeoning herself against it.

Just as Ridley was about to concede a woman appeared, clad in nondescript apparel with bright, loose hair. Her eyes were a sort of molten gold, and they didn't linger.

"Afternoon, are you having some trouble?"

Friday whipped around, so busy letting out her frustration she'd not seen the other woman approach.

"Oh... uh... a bit. The door's stuck."

Ridley bit back a smile; watching a flustered Friday was a rare but enjoyable sight.

The other woman came closer. "I'm not surprised. I've lived here all my life and never known this place to be anything but empty. Do you mind?" She gestured to the door, and at Ridley's nod Friday moved aside. The woman placed her hands against the wood, long, tapered fingers pressing hard. "The wood's warped."

"Told you." Friday smirked, satisfaction coated in the grime now smudged down one side of her.

Ridley traced it with her eyes. "You smell like dirt."

Friday let out an indignant squawk, grabbing at the Shadow, who danced away laughing.

The golden woman paused, a small smile tugging at her lips. "I can set it right if you like? Reshape the wood."

Friday nodded. "It won't tax you too much?"

"I shouldn't think so."

"Well, if you wouldn't mind."

"Of course." The stranger smiled; without turning she raised her hand behind her, fingertip merely brushing the old wood. A gentle groan wavered through the air before it abruptly stopped. "All done."

Ridley picked up their bags, moving to stand by the door. She gave it a light push and it swung open, hinges creaking. She turned to the stranger. "Thank you…"

"Roman."

"Ridley, and this is Friday."

Roman nodded to the both of them, shifting so that Friday could peer inside the lonely tower.

"Looks as though you've both got a fair bit of work ahead of you."

Friday grumbled. "Apparently so."

"If you need any help, don't hesitate to ask me." Roman gave them a parting grin before turning to go, Friday calling after her.

"Where will we find you?"

Roman cast a glance over her shoulder. "The Highfort."

When Ridley turned to go inside Friday's expression stopped her; she couldn't quite tell if the other was happy or horrified.

"Friday?"

"We just met our first Greycoat." She looked to where Roman's figure had last been.

"She didn't seem so bad."

"No, I guess not." Friday turned to her, smouldering fire back in her eyes. "Now." She pulled Ridley into the tower, kicking the door shut behind them. "I believe you said something about not needing a bed."

Chapter 7

SMOKE

The meeting was not going well; Watt really shouldn't have brought Modesto with him. He'd thought safety in numbers, he and his oldest friend side by side against those that would seek to harm them. But then they'd sat opposite Shine and Stone, and Watt's confidence waned under their unspoken authority.

They were, both of them, very much as their names implied: Stone an unreadable goliath of a woman and Shine every inch the politician. She wasn't voted in for her frankness or scruples, but for her charm; she was the smiling face of a prosperous city. Often Watt contemplated what should happen when the bubble inevitably burst, when the good times failed. It was why he voted against her, but the masses had spoken.

Beside him Modesto vibrated, his bandaged left hand fidgeting against the armrest.

Shine cleared her throat. "Andromeda's reports, I'm afraid, have been less than favourable."

Traitor, Watt thought; after he'd been so welcoming, he'd even made her tea.

"So what," he struggled to keep his voice level, "does that mean exactly?"

"Well, it's not the most promising of starts, Watterson, I can't lie; not a promising start at all."

Modesto grunted. "It's a working factory; prototypes, machines. Accidents happen."

Stone glanced at Modesto's hand, and once again Watt regretted bringing him. "Just how many accidents have you been in, Cinnabar, since the funeral?"

Watt's mind tripped; Stone had a point. Modesto had always been somewhat oblivious to safety in the workshop, but recently...

Green eyes, reddish dark hair, freckles. And a baby face. Which in and of itself wouldn't have been a problem, but then there were the twig-like limbs and, of course, the fact that the bottle-green gaze barely reached his collarbone. By the Mother–

"Ash, a word." He stalked outside, ignoring his friend's hurried placations and scowling at the city before him.

"What's the matter?"

"Ash, that boy is a boy."

Ash blinked, giving Watt that look, the one that so often led to an argument he was bound to lose.

Watt huffed. "What I mean is, he's a child."

"I don't think–"

"I'm not a child."

Hands on his bony hips and wearing a pout that obviously wanted to be something else, Modesto wasn't doing himself any favours.

Watt scoffed. "How old are you then, boy?"

"Seventeen."

"There, see?"

"Ash Marty Sevo, this boy is not seventeen." Watt frowned down at said boy, who refused to wilt. "You're twelve tops."

Modesto sputtered, "I'm fourteen, you arse!"

"Yes, that's more like it." Watt looked at Ash, who, as per usual, didn't appear in the least troubled by the revelation. Watt sighed, body deflating. "We can't just take a child home, let alone have him in an actual workshop."

"Course we can."

It was as if all the gears in his head screeched to a stop all at once, crunching his brain as it flaked off bits of rust.

"Excuse me?"

"We'll just have to look after him."

"We'll just what?"

"I don't need looking after."

Ash's heavy hand landed on one of Modesto's birdy shoulders, his stalk legs nearly buckling. Watt fought the urge to smile. Up until last spring Ash has still been a gangly thing; though he'd always looked full of the potential to grow as he had. Modesto had a touch of the runt about him. Watt threw off the growing fondness.

"We're starting a business, we can't be responsible for a child and we definitely can't put him in charge of heavy machinery."

"I don't see why not."

"You fucking… boy, where are your parents?"

Modesto answered, casual as could be, "In Harleon." There went Watt's brain again.

"Harleon?"

"Uh..." Finally trepidation had crept into Ash's voice, those natural protective instincts pulling at his brows. "Do they know where you are? Wait, did you have to leave them–"

Modesto's tinny little laugh cut through Ash's frantic tirade, the noise not half as annoying as Watt wanted it to be.

"No, they sent me here to go to school."

Watt frowned again; this kid was going to give him wrinkles. "And you aren't there because...?"

"I don't like it. 'Cause I'm not magic they treat me like I'm stupid – what do I want to learn to cook for? I don't want no babies and I don't want to teach anyone else's either."

"I see."

Watt looked at Ash, seeing resolve settle in those hazel eyes. Well, it looked like the lost boy was theirs now. This twiglet from Harleon was going to be trouble; he could feel it in his bones.

"All right, fine, but when the Children's League come asking why we've got him in your house without his parents' knowledge you can deal with them." He turned to Ash, ignoring the tall man's exuberant smile. "And you're looking after him too..."

"No more than usual." Ash could hear the tension in his friend's voice, see it in the set of his shoulders; this really wasn't going well.

Shine clasped her hands in front of her, the epitome of patience. "According to our reports, *you* have made up half of the accidents yourself, Modesto."

Watt looked at his partner, feeling his heart race. He refused to give in to the panicking voice in the back of his mind; the one that would tear them in two. Watt needed Modesto now more than ever; his friend's bad temper and anguish aside, he couldn't do without him.

He jumped in. "Nothing to worry about, Governor, I assure you, just a few teething problems. Ash was in charge of safety, you see; tragically ironic, don't you think?" Watt could feel Modesto's confused frown boring into the side of his face; it was no matter, though. He'd managed to make Shine uncomfortable, pique her pity just enough. Perhaps he could get through this morning after all.

"Yes, yes, of course; I perfectly understand, Watterson." Over Shine's shoulder he saw Stone's brow twitch; thank the gods she wasn't in charge of the governor. "As you say, you just need a little more time to sort yourselves out."

"In which case," Stone's voice hit like an anvil, and she stared Watt down, "I suggest you take extra care, Cinnabar's no more indestructible than Sevo was, Teach."

His hand shot out to Modesto's arm, fingers squeezing just enough to keep his friend in his seat. Watt hated the way those words sunk in, etching themselves into his bones for the rest of his life; he could nearly hear the scraping.

He cleared his throat. "Thank you, Commissioner, your words are duly noted." Reluctantly he took his hand from his friend's arm, glancing back to Shine, who looked wholly disturbed by the proceedings. "If that'll be all, Governor, we'd like to get back to Wes."

"Yes, yes, of course, Watterson. Do make sure the boy returns to school in a timely manner, won't you? Besides that, you're welcome to go."

With the sharpest nod he could manage, he up and left, Modesto close behind. He'd not dared to look at Stone as they were dismissed, too afraid of what she might say, of what she'd already said.

As soon as they were out of earshot he rounded on the other man. "Are you trying to shut us down?"

Modesto looked astonished, green eyes wide.

"I don't know what you think you're playing at–"

"Playing at?"

"But it needs to stop."

"I've not done anything."

Watt snatched at Modesto's left hand, where his middle and index fingers had been strapped together to set the bone.

"Then what is this, Modesto?" He ignored the other's grimace, pulling him in closer. "How many accidents have you had in the past week? How many more times am I meant to put you back together before it's not enough?"

With his blood pounding so fast and so loud Watt unconsciously pulled the other man even closer, the answering pained yelp startling him so badly he recoiled as if struck. When he took stock, Modesto was cradling his damaged hand to his chest, staring at Watt as if he'd never seen him before. It made his heart stutter.

"Mods–"

"I'm sorry."

Watt blinked – perhaps he'd imagined the whole thing and he hadn't just hurt his oldest friend. Or perhaps he had, and the reality was worse, because Modesto was apologising for it.

"I'm just… I'm sorry."

Watt's heart caught in his throat, tasting bitter and acrid. "Don't be sorry, Mods." He approached slowly, marvelling as the other man remained in place. When he raised his hand to cup Modesto's neck and he didn't flinch, Watt's worries melted away. He'd not broken them. "I don't want you to be sorry." He leant in, gently guiding Modesto to do the same till their foreheads touched; warmth shared once more. "I want you to be careful."

They took a walk through the town, forgoing the streetcar for a chance to clear their heads in the rare sunshine. Watt frowned at how gingerly Modesto still cradled his hand, but he kept quiet; his friend wouldn't take the fuss.

"Watt?"

Watt stopped, turning to find the other a few steps behind; he hadn't noticed him slow.

"Yes?"

Modesto bit his lip, giving his hand an experimental twitch before going on. "Why did you tell them Ash was in charge of safety at the factory?"

He should have seen it coming, but the question was still a hurtful surprise.

"It was just to get us out of there, I knew Shine would get uncomfortable if we mentioned Ash."

"Oh."

There were times Watt forgot Modesto was the youngest of them, that he'd been little more than a boy when he and Ash had recruited him. Only when his friend was unsure, when Modesto's voice sounded small and far off, was Watt reminded of it.

"There was no malice to it, Mods, it was just the simpler option."

"I know, I just… I don't…" He trailed off, Watt waiting patiently for Modesto to sort himself out. He wished he understood how that mind worked; that mind that made such wondrous things. Gradually, he continued, "I might go back to the mansion."

Watt blinked. "Oh?"

"I'm tired."

"That's all?"

"Of course." The smile Watt received was unsure, and he felt it hit deep down. Perhaps, and it pained him to think it, he'd done more damage than he thought.

As much as Watt wanted to go with Modesto, to fix things, he could tell his presence wouldn't be welcome. The other man was holding his damaged hand like a shield, and as he slowly wandered off Watt couldn't help but watch him go.

He was alone, hands twitching and breath catching; he was on his own and he hated it. He thought of Wes, no doubt with Leon watching everyone work; he should get back to the boy, and yet…

He turned away from the way back, letting his feet carry him where they would. People passed by in a blur, voices and faces melding to nothing as he went on. In his mind all he could see was Modesto, staring at him like a stranger – what would Wes say? What would Ash have said?

Suddenly a shout burst through the haze, a hand coming to land on his shoulder.

"Dad?" It was Evie, staring at him with shining brown eyes and a merry smile. He stared mutely at her for a moment, still half in his own head. "Everything all right? I didn't think you ever came here."

That caught his notice, and slowly he took stock of his surroundings. The crowds of people, mishmash of buildings and indecipherable sounds of so many talking at once; by the Mother, he hated the Rise.

He turned back to Evie, who looked on him now with concern. "Are you all right?"

Watt frowned. "Not particularly."

She grabbed his hand, leading him away from the crowded plaza till they found an isolated bench by a small, blossoming pink tree.

When they sat she turned to him, gaze earnest. "What's happened?"

Where to begin? He was suddenly so tired. "I just had a meeting with Shine and Stone..."

Evie's brow darkened; her malice reminded him so much of her mother.

"It would seem the governor and commissioner aren't happy with the reports they've been getting."

"If that Andromeda Knight is causing you trouble–"

"I appreciate the sentiment, Evie, but you getting involved in this won't help anyone."

She huffed, glaring out at the crowd.

"Besides, I heard her telling Wes she's impervious to harm, so your usual tactics wouldn't do much good."

Evie's laugh warmed his chest, the sound just as it'd always been. If only all his troubles could be solved so easily.

"Seriously though, Dad, if you're in trouble I can help. These magics can't just throw their weight around the second one of our lot starts doing well."

"It's not that I don't agree with you, it's just..." He thought of Modesto again, and blood and fire and pictures of Ash; all they had left of him now. They should have taken more care. "I'm afraid they've a point this time. Ash died; he died and now Modesto is chipping away at himself bit by bit and I can't get Wes to go back to school or anywhere at all–"

"Dad. Dad, breathe."

He took in a breath, only just realising how desperately he needed one; Evie's hand a comforting weight on his shoulder.

"Would you like to hear my opinion?"

"Always."

"I think you're perfectly capable of sorting your issues yourself. Them looming over you and making threats is the trouble here." That conviction in her voice served her well, rallied people to her, but he wouldn't ask her to rally them to him.

"You're right, as always. It's just a shame Commissioner Stone refuses to agree."

The smirk she sent him rattled his bones; her mother was before him again. "Don't worry about Stone, Dad, she just needs her attention drawn elsewhere."

"Evie, what have you done?"

Chapter 8

BLACK AND BLUE

It was nice to go out on her own; Lara never thought she'd say that. She never thought she'd get a chance to do it. Yet there she was, strolling through Cerrano alone, utilising her free time – she still gawked at the term. Free time; how Hadren had laughed at Lara's expression – she had to laugh, she'd said, or she might 'just fucking cry'. It seemed as though Lara was doing no good for Bound's reputation, and she might just like that more than this whole 'free time' business. Wander, Roman had said, she should go for a wander; it was a nice word. Sort of soft and songlike; wandering could only be an enjoyable thing.

She couldn't totally escape herself, though, and as much as she'd like to wander she'd also come out with a mission in mind: clothes, or her lack thereof. Lara was on the lookout for things that looked nice, fabrics or styles she wanted for herself. She'd only her uniform, and it wouldn't do for wandering.

She ended up in the mess that was Market Town, the constant noise and stream of people such a new sight she had to pause on the threshold. The things she'd done, that she'd had, were always such bland affairs that to behold the cacophony of sights and smells sent her head into a whirl. She'd gotten so much wrong in the past three weeks, confused by anything and everything, that she didn't want to assume. Hadren didn't seem to mind telling her anything, but she'd rather figure things out herself; apparently that was half the fun.

Weaving through the people, she kept an eye on their dress; colours and styles she'd always wanted, dangling things that shone or clinked together. She liked those, the pretty little additions with no purpose to them whatsoever. The thought made her smile; it'd be nice to own something, for it to be hers; for no reason but that she thought it pretty. She pondered – what made something pretty? It wasn't a conscious thing, she didn't set out to find something and deem it as such; she just saw something and thought, *That's pretty.* Was she pretty, or the market vendor with the fruit, or Hadren or Roman? Hadren, maybe, it suited Hadren. Roman, though, she was something else, something with a different ring to it; there was a word out there to describe Roman Ion, Lara just had to find it. Perhaps, she thought to herself, she'd discover it amongst the fragrant, chaotic stalls, or maybe she wouldn't. Lara decided to try all the same.

Piles of colour caught her eye; stacks upon stacks of cloth, various hues and patterns just waiting to be desired. She approached slowly, eyes widening to take them all in. She ran a finger across a purple fold, the fabric softer than anything she'd ever been told to wear. Moving up, she felt reds and pinks in shades holding names she'd never heard, crafted expertly and handled with care. Then her eyes found it: a corner of blue she'd dreamed of. Gently Lara pulled it out of its hiding place, running her fingers along the sparse, soft golden patterns woven into the sapphire sheet.

She looked to the vendor. "How much for this?"

The woman peered at Lara. "Four crowns, ten florins. Special price for a Greycoat."

"All right. Thank you." Lara swiftly handed the money over, hesitating only at the strange look on the other's face. "Is there a problem?"

The vendor shook her head. "Oh, no; no problem at all. I'll just wrap that up for you. Make sure it's safe and sound."

Lara kept the parcel close to her chest, fingers crinkling the paper in a quest to feel a trace of the loveliness within. She couldn't help her smile; it was nice to own something. In her musings she strolled by a small group, pausing only when she caught a snatch of their conversation.

"…Just coming round here. You need to fuck off back behind your walls."

She backed up, manoeuvring till she could see who the disgruntled-looking group were staring at.

It was a woman, just a girl really, barely older than Lara by look alone. She'd skin a sort of golden brown and heavy eyebrows; even from a distance Lara could make them out. The stranger was also clad in the traditional purple-and-white garb of the Citadel envoys; Lara had been ignored by them on many occasions. Whatever was going on the woman was outnumbered, though she didn't appear worried; none of the telltale signs Lara detected so easily. Suddenly their eyes met, and those eyebrows climbed.

"Officer, perfect timing."

The mob turned, panic in their eyes growing upon catching sight of Lara.

She cleared her throat. "Is there a problem?" She straightened up, holding her precious cargo safely by her side. One of the group, a man in a fine suit, came forward.

"We've started no trouble, Officer. But this *woman* came down here making remarks–"

"I did no such thing, I can assure you. It was they who set upon me."

Lara tilted her head, gaze trailing slowly from the group to the lone figure, who still looked unmoved by the situation. She stepped toward Lara, bringing with her the scents of paper and steam.

"Apparently magical folk aren't welcome in Market Town."

Lara frowned. "I see."

A snort erupted from the group, a large man pushing his way forward and squaring up to Lara.

"That's right, and we bloody well meant it." The suited man grabbed at him, but he scoffed at their concerns. "So fucking what, she's a Greycoat. We know all about your kind, so reliant on magic your minds rot in it. Too thick to function otherwise."

She wouldn't recoil, though his breath was warm and moist on her face and he kept trying to loom over her; Greycoats did not back down. The people of Bound did not back down.

"Stupid, arrogant cunts, the lot of you. Your time's over, that's what they say, it's our go now. The world's outgrown you."

Those words caught her attention, an eloquent spark in a crude machine; not his own, she was certain. Lara scanned the mob as he continued, spying leaflets in each of their hands.

"I'm fucking talking to you!" The man snatched at her, succeeding in grabbing the package still wrapped so neatly in her hands. With a pull, the sound of tearing paper and fabric alike split the air.

Lara's world sharpened to his grubby hand, clutching and dirtying the only nice thing she'd ever owned. Her heartbeat pounded through her ears like a war drum, fury a wild dance in her muscles. Her trainers had always said her intent painted her features a darker colour, and it seemed the man could see them clear as day as he backed away. She dropped the ruined cloth, revelling in the way the crowd parted in fear; prey always tasted sweeter when scared. It was over before it really began, Lara wasting no time in flinging herself into the fray in a righteous flurry of supernatural strength and finely-honed reflexes. The sound of snapping bone was a symphony she'd missed, and by the time she was done the mob and their leaflets were prostrate on the ground. Gradually her breathing slowed, the erratic pulsing in her head diminishing till all was as it had been before.

Someone cleared their throat. Turning, she caught sight of the envoy, holding Lara's ruined package out to her.

"Here, some of it can still be saved."

Lara took it reverently, running her hands over the dirtied, fraying edges. "Thank you."

"I think I ought to be saying that, really. I'm Andromeda Knight."

"Lara Key." A groan returned her attention to the indisposed group lying about, and she stepped over them to pick up a leaflet. A quick glance at it revealed all. "Anti-magic propaganda. These liberationists are everywhere."

Andromeda smiled at her, eyes trailing over her in a way Lara had never felt before. "I suppose that type of dissension isn't a problem in Bound."

"No type of dissension is a problem in Bound."

Andromeda hummed. "Well, I'm from Berra, so trust me when I say this will only get worse. Especially after your… display of strength."

Looking around her, Lara realised what Andromeda had meant; perhaps her trainers had been right after all.

"I should report back, tell the commander about this." She held up the leaflet. "And this." She winced as she gestured at the people, some of whom were beginning to stir.

"I'll come with you if you like, be a witness? I did get you into it after all."

"Thank you."

"It's the least I can do. I'm sorry about your fabric too – were you trying to make something for an occasion?"

Lara looked down at the blue, still so startling even covered in dirt.

"Uh, no, I just… just wanted to have some clothes that weren't a uniform."

"Oh, of course you do. How long since you left Bound?"

"Just over three weeks."

Andromeda made a strange little noise in her throat, nodding as she pulled Lara's arm to loop with hers.

"I'll help you get some more, after we report in? Make sure none of these traders try to cheat you."

Lara finally understood the look on that vendor's face earlier; at least Hadren hadn't been there to see her fail again.

As they walked away Lara really looked Andromeda over, rolling the name around her mouth. Those expressive, heavy brows were flecked with all shades of brown, even a little blue hidden in there. Beneath were a pair of deep indigo eyes, slightly mismatched but all the better for it. Staring at her, Lara could only think one thing: *Pretty.*

Chapter 9

ALCHEMY

From the back Ridley could hear Friday talking, that rumbling tenor making its way to her as she dealt and chatted with the masses. She remembered a ghost of that feeling, the excitement of meeting someone new. Of course, she couldn't have that now. More voices rolled in, all of them expressing the same astonishment that after all these years the clock tower was alive again. Ridley chuckled to imagine the face Friday must be making, shoulders set and brows twitching; she'd never had the patience for small talk.

Ridley focused back on the table, eyes tracing over the gears strewn about. Tiny pieces of bronze and copper just waiting to be put back together, her hands moving with utmost care as she worked.

"By Io Sola, when will it end?" Friday was clutching the door frame, a look of despair about her.

Ridley shifted some gears as she spoke. "We've only been open two days, Friday."

"Lyra wept, is that all? These monsters are draining the life out of me."

"They're customers, love, not monsters."

"Oh, I wasn't aware there was a difference."

She heard Friday saunter closer, draping herself over Ridley's back like a downy blanket; heavy and warm and content to be supported completely.

Ridley huffed. "Do you mind?"

"Not at all."

After a few minutes of contented silence, wherein the parts in Ridley's hands finally started to resemble something, Friday shifted. Her breath, which had been so warm and tingling against Ridley's neck, travelled up to her ear, a full-body shiver coursing through her. Sharp teeth nipped at the shell, a clever tongue quickly following to soothe the sting.

Ridley hissed, "Friday, I'm trying to work."

"Why?"

"To make money." Those lips trailed a warm, wet path down to her neck, where they instantly latched on to a patch of skin. After a particularly hard bite, Ridley's back arched. "Ah, Friday–"

"You can just make us some money."

"And… uh… what happened to… to staying on the right side of the law?" One of Friday's hands crawled over Ridley's hips, moving to rub insistently at the heat between her legs. "Oh–"

"It was a good plan, but I'd rather fuck."

"Hello?"

Friday groaned. "For fuck's sake."

Ridley forced a calm breath as the other woman stopped her ministrations. "Friday–"

"Kiss first."

Ridley turned her head, Friday's eager eyes watching each and every shift. She leant in and pecked the other woman on the corner of the mouth, the barest brush against Friday's pouting lips.

"Off you go."

Friday was indignant. "That was not a kiss, Ridley Ripley."

"You get what you earn."

The older woman threw up her hands, finally tearing herself away to go. "Bloody tease, you'll pay for this later."

Ridley smiled wistfully, feeling the heat fade from her spine with each step Friday took, though that warmth remained low in her belly. She shook her head clear of those desires, focusing once again on her work as her lover's voice drifted in through the open door. As she fiddled with some small pieces a shadow fell across the table, her peace falling away as she looked up and beheld not Friday, but a stranger. The woman was looking at her with an attempt at nonchalance, blue eyes flitting about the room but always finding their way back to Ridley.

She kept her face blank. "Customers aren't allowed back here."

"I do apologise."

Ridley held in the rebuke, the woman's words sounding lazy and insincere. Turning back to her work, she ignored the other's continued presence; however the sound of steps gave her cause to look up.

"What are you doing?" The stranger had moved further into the room, staring at the mess of spare and broken things as she went. She was steadfastly looking away from Ridley, but the Shadow knew where her attention was fixed.

The woman spoke offhandedly. "There's a story about this clock tower."

Ridley bit back her groan. "I've no care to hear it."

"They say a Shadow built it."

Ridley frowned, glancing to the door in hope, but she could still hear Friday chatting in the front.

"I'd always thought it to be nonsense; what would someone like you be doing building clocks, surely you've better things to be doing with your time?"

Ridley bristled, that old, familiar dread seeping in. "You'll find stories have little grounding in reality."

"Stories about your kind most of all." The way the woman looked at her, with a hunger made of greed more than need, set Ridley's teeth on edge.

"I've told you once, you aren't allowed back here. Please leave."

The stranger smiled. "I'm merely being friendly."

"I've no need of friends."

The woman made a tutting sound. "Everyone needs friends, especially in a city like this." She came around the bench, leaning into Ridley's space, but Ridley wouldn't be moved. "Someone like you needs all the friends they can get."

The word 'Shadow' had been spat at Ridley so often, in so foul a manner, that to have this woman not deign to utter it was like a kick to the chest. The stranger's smile was sickeningly saccharine as she inched closer, hand coming up to toy with a loose strand of Ridley's hair.

In an instant she was yanked back, clasping her wrist and staring over Ridley's shoulder.

Out rang a voice the Shadow knew all too well. "On your way." She turned to find Friday at the door, face as calm as could be.

The stranger straightened, fixing the cuff of her sleeve. "Terribly sorry, I wasn't aware I couldn't come back here." If Ridley had been younger she was sure she'd be surprised at the gall, but she'd seen enough of people to know better.

Friday's voice was level. "You know now." A calm Friday was a volatile thing; even the other woman seemed to realise as she held up her hands in surrender.

"I apologise again. I'll go." She turned at the door to glance at Ridley once more in that same ravenous manner, then nodded to Friday. "Good day."

As the steps of her retreat faded Ridley felt herself slipping, sensation falling away till her own breaths were heavy against her tongue and rattled on their way down. She scratched against the worktop but felt nothing, all the world shrinking around her. A hand yanked hard on her hair, grip so tight it made her scalp ache. She leant in to it, sighing at the feeling as the hand loosened its grip and cradled her head.

"You with me, girl?" Friday's face swam into focus, so close Ridley counted the lashes around her left eye. She was drowned in sensation; in Friday's touch, her smell, the colours in her eyes and hair, till Ridley was safely back to herself. Back to Friday.

"I'm with you, Friday." She winced, glancing down to see her fingertips bloody and torn. "Ow."

Friday used her leverage on Ridley's hair to pull her up and in tight against her, slotting perfectly with the Shadow's face tucked into her neck.

Ridley mumbled, "You were right."

Friday's continued ministrations on her scalp were making her sleepy, as was the soft tone of her voice. "About what?"

"We've should've just fucked."

Friday laughed. "There's no *just* about it." Her breath was hot on Ridley's forehead, and the Shadow could hear the other woman's pulse under her ear like a lullaby.

"She'll come back, you know."

Friday tightened her hold, crushing cotton and hair in her grasp. "Then I'll kill her."

Chapter 10

SHOSHANNA

She'd eyes like his, bright brown and framed by short, thick lashes, left one ever so slightly tilted. No one would notice unless he pointed it out; he should know, after all. She was the same dusty brown as him too, but the tuft of hair on her head was light, almost brassy, just like Evelyn's.

"She looks like you."

"I'm shocked you can tell from all the way over there."

Modesto snorted, lips quivering to smile as he scooted closer.

"You want to hold her, Mods?"

"Uh…"

Watt held back the mirth that bubbled in his chest. Watching the boy struggle with pleasantries hadn't lessened in hilarity over the two years they'd known him.

"No thanks, I'm fairly certain I don't like babies."

"Says the baby."

"Hey!"

A gurgle burst forth from the little thing in Watt's arms, a not-quite-smile on that tiny mouth.

"Don't you worry none, sweetheart, Modesto will love you just as much as you love him soon enough."

Ash's arrival stopped anything the young man was going to say, a whirlwind of energy scooping up the baby before Watt could blink.

"Hey, titch, did you miss your Uncle Ash? Did you?"

Watt could just picture his daughter's face, staring up at those big hazel eyes in awe.

"Of course she did, Uncle Modesto won't play with her. Or get within a foot of her."

Ash grinned, cradling the baby close as he approached the boy. "Aw, is little Modesto scared of a baby?"

"Just for that, you can design your own streetcar. I happen to like walking – stop grinning at me!"

"What? I have a lovely smile."

Watt chuckled. "Yes, lovely like a shark."

Ash pouted, leaning in to a little ear and stage-whispering conspiracies. "Your daddy's so mean."

Watt smiled as his oldest friend continued to rock his new daughter gently, her body looking even tinier in his big hands.

"Where's Evelyn?"

Watt blinked, turning to find Modesto closer than he had been in days. The boy ran warm as he leant in; he hadn't realised he'd missed it.

"Sorry?"

"Evelyn, I haven't seen her about at all, come to think of it."

"Oh, she was… uh… called in."

Modesto frowned, and Watt couldn't help but marvel at the way his freckles shifted. "But it's only been a few days."

Watt shrugged. "Called in, went in, what's the difference? She's doing her duty and I'm doing mine."

"I see."

They were silent for a few moments, watching Ash singing softly to the gurgling little bundle in his arms.

"What if she gets sent to the line? There's rumblings over in Myrana again."

Watt held his breath, stomach plummeting. He felt the moment it clicked for Modesto; the boy's shoulders falling into his.

"Oh, I'm sorry."

"Don't be, we each have our gods to follow." Warmth flowed into him; here was this young man, this boy offering him comfort, and all Watt could do was marvel over how sweet he smelled.

"You named her yet?" Ash was staring at them, face no doubt inscrutable to Modesto, but Watt knew they'd be arguing later.

"Yes."

"It's not–"

"It is."

Ash growled, placing the baby in Modesto's unwilling arms.

"Ash!"

"Name her what you want, Watt, but leave Queen and country out of it. She doesn't deserve–"

"Evelyn is her mother."

"Barely."

Fussing sounded beside Watt, his tension draining away at the sight of Modesto shushing his newborn daughter as gently as he did his machines.

"Look, she likes Mods. She can't be an Evelyn."

Watt smiled. "No, she's an Evie."

Evie, from her first day out in the world, had a habit of picking up the less favourably looked upon creatures. Never had a girl had so many pet spiders – or pigeons. Even her friends had been less than stellar at first glance. This new one, though, Watt was rather unsure what to make of her. He'd seen Shoshanna of course, up on the platform with his daughter; a little less zeal than Evie, but plenty of charm in its stead. She was neat, shirt crisp and nails perfect; not Evie's usual type of comrade at all.

He looked down at her plate, completely free of anything, cutlery still sat on either side; only the tea touched her lips.

"Feel free to help yourself, no need to stand on ceremony in this house."

Powdery blue eyes flickered to meet him, an easy smile beneath. "That's very kind of you, but I worry my mother's ghost would rise up should I start without everyone here."

"Particular on manners, was she?"

"Extremely."

A loud crunch came from down the table, Evie licking the toast crumbs from her fingertips as she chewed.

Watt sighed. "Apparently I was rather lax in that area." His daughter smiled, as did Wes, who was simultaneously trying to stuff as many strawberries into his mouth as humanly possible.

Evie laughed. "Just showing my appreciation, Dad. Not like Mods gives a damn anyway."

Before he could respond, steps precluded the very man's entrance, who stopped short when he noticed them all staring.

"Uh, good morning."

Evie waved. "Morning, Mods. This is Shoshanna."

Modesto nodded at her, shifting from foot to foot.

Shoshanna spoke up. "May I just say, it's an honour to meet the man who built both the streetcar *and* the royal fleet's newest guns."

Watt grimaced, staring silently as Modesto's shoulders hunched in.

"I just designed them..."

Watt stood slowly. "We've been waiting to start breakfast – well, some of us have." His chest hurt as his friend's eyes tracked him but refused to meet his. "Are you hungry?"

"I've got to take Wes to school – what in Io Sola are you doing?"

Watt followed Modesto's sputtering to Wes, whose cheeks were bulging as he struggled to chew everything he'd shoved in his mouth. The boy responded with a sound so muffled by squished food Modesto could only frown.

"What?"

"He's trying to see how many strawberries he can fit in his mouth. I think he got nine." Evie looked to Wes, who nodded, still frowning determinedly as he chewed.

"Wes, when you're done choking yourself we need to go. We're late enough as it is."

Watt watched as the young boy nodded, jumping up and moving to Modesto.

"Swallow first." It was nice to see some of his friend's fire again, even if it wasn't directed at him.

Wes turned back to them all, wide, pink-tinted teeth on full display as he smiled. "Bye." He left, Modesto following and muttering about the cost of fruit.

Watt groaned, slumping back into his chair and hearing his bones creak. A flying piece of cheese suddenly hit him squarely between the eyes, with a huff he looked at Evie. She was glaring at him.

"What've you done?"

"I recall asking you that question a few days ago."

"Don't change the subject. What's wrong with Modesto?"

"It's just a period of adjustment, for all of us. He's struggling." Watt hated himself, hearing lies drip off his tongue so easily; when had he learned to do that?

"What happened to his hand?" Shoshanna was staring at him, plate still empty.

"He broke it."

Evie cut in. "I thought it was just fractured."

"It was." Watt fought down bile – no wonder Modesto wouldn't come near him. He shook his head, sitting up and forcing himself to take some food. "No one to wait for now. Enjoy."

They ate peacefully for a few minutes, until the sad spectre of Modesto had faded enough for Watt to remember why he'd wanted the two women over in the first place. "So, Evie told me some of your plans."

Shoshanna paused, glancing from daughter to father. "Did she?"

"Yes, about the literature and the rallies and whatnot."

"I've been telling Dad about the cause, and how the syndicate's become an example for the liberationists."

"True; what you, Cinnabar and Sevo have done is nothing short of groundbreaking in Gallow. You've really helped lend credibility to our cause."

Watt looked at them both, shifting in his seat. "I appreciate that, but it wasn't intentional. We do still hire magical people."

The smile Shoshanna sent him was bright. "All causes start somewhere. And it's not that we're against magics in any way–"

"We just want to be their equals." Evie stabbed a piece of potato, the sound of metal meeting ceramic grating at his nerves. "We're not asking much."

Watt took a bite of his own, letting the rich saltiness take over his senses for a few moments. They both looked so grave. Swallowing, he replied, "It's not that I don't support your cause, I'd be a fool not to. But our situation at the moment is far too precarious for us to start getting political. How exactly can you help us?"

Shoshanna took a slow sip of tea before replying, "We want their attention. You don't."

"I see. So this mass march Evie told me about, it's just the start, then?"

Evie nodded. "They won't have the time to stare over your shoulder once we get started."

It all made sense, but Watt heard a little voice crying at the back of his skull; it sounded an awful lot like Ash. "No one will get hurt, though; you won't get hurt?" He looked at Evie, watching for any sign of reluctance or fear, but she was content.

"Trust me, Dad, violence isn't what we're about."

"No. We leave that to the magics."

Watt frowned at Shoshanna, who was looking down at her cup like it could bite. He cleared his throat. "What do you mean? Have you had some trouble?"

"Some of our members were attacked by a Greycoat a few days ago; completely unprovoked of course."

"She set upon them like a wild animal."

Shoshanna looked at him. "They were healed, but the fact remains that she's not even been reprimanded..." She cut herself off, looking for all the world like she was containing herself.

"Greycoats have always been known for that sort of behaviour." Watt spoke sadly. "Their only hand is a heavy one."

Shoshanna sat back, sighing deeply and worrying her lip. It was Evie who went on, however.

"And there's what happened yesterday."

Watt looked between them. "What happened?"

"Shoshanna was harassed by a metal-twister."

"Where?"

The woman in question shook her head. "The clock tower in the Old District. It finally has some owners so we went to see and, well..."

"The twister attacked her."

Watt frowned darkly. "Did they give any explanation for it?"

Evie cried out, eyes wide, "It was because of a Shadow."

Watt balked. "A *Shadow*?"

Shoshanna looked dejected. "It was all a misunderstanding. I caught a glimpse of the Shadow in the back and just thought I'd be welcoming. It didn't seem right to have her kept back there alone..."

"You can hardly have her out with everyone."

"Evie," Watt glared at his daughter, "I thought I raised you better than that at least."

"Come on, Dad, fancy protecting a Shadow from someone when we all know what they're capable of."

Did they? Watt remembered the stories, but he'd never met anyone who'd come face-to-face with a Shadow before. Maybe, he thought, they weren't quite so frightening after all. At least this one didn't seem to be.

"Anyway," Shoshanna continued, "it was all just a misunderstanding."

Watt watched silently as they continued their conversation, mind whirring as he took it all in. He couldn't lie to himself and pretend getting the Citadel off their backs wouldn't be a relief, but the cost seemed too little. He looked at Evie, that idealism no doubt clouding her judgement. Did she really comprehend what having the Citadel's attention would mean? Or the Greycoats, for that matter? He peered at Shoshanna, who, compared to Evie's animated gestures, was the epitome of composure. Perhaps she'd be the even keel to his daughter's fire. Watt glanced down at her empty plate, frowning. He noted the way her perfectly clean fingernails drummed succinctly against the table, at once calm and impatient.

Chapter 11

UNBECOMING

Jackie wasn't pleased; Lara could see it in the way she marched about, shutting herself in her office for hours on end. She wouldn't admit to being worried – concerned perhaps, but not worried. Lara had no idea what the matter could be; if anything things had seemed rather sedate as of late. Which was why, upon being summoned to the commander's office to be greeted with a look of displeasure, she couldn't quite contain her surprise. She sat when Jackie gestured, hands clutched loosely in her lap and fingers twitching.

The commander stared her down. "We need to talk about the incident that occurred exactly nine days ago."

"Incident?"

"In Market Town."

Oh, she'd forgotten about that.

"What about it, Commander?"

Jackie cleared her throat, the sound echoing about the

chamber. "Your actions were unbecoming of a respectable Greycoat."

Lara frowned, going over the events in her mind. She'd subdued the offenders, done no lasting damage, defended Andromeda and informed the Citadel of inflammatory propaganda – what was so unbecoming?

"I'm… I'm afraid I don't understand, Commander."

"You don't?"

An uncomfortable silence fell, but Lara waited it out.

"I've had a look at your notes, Key, the ones that came with you from Bound." Lara cringed, heart sinking. "I should have looked sooner, put you with a more experienced partner."

What? "Pardon, ma'am?"

Jackie pulled out a hefty file, flicking through the pages whilst Lara looked on in anguish. "For all of Cadet Gogh's amiable qualities she lacks the ability to instil order, although that seems to be a trait found in most Cerranites."

Lara couldn't have that; the indignation was running up her spine.

"May I speak, ma'am?" Jackie gestured for her to go on. "To be fair to Had… Cadet Gogh, she's my partner, not my superior. And she wasn't with me at the time in question." It was her free time – she still loved the taste of those words.

"No, you were on free time according to your report." Once again the commander looked down at the folder, deft hands sifting. "You were put on a lot of extra exercises by the looks of it."

Exercises, the exercises; *run, run, run till your legs give out.* Lara ran a finger across her knuckles, catching the grooves of long-healed breaks.

"Do you feel you benefited from this extra discipline?"

She thought of mud and rain, of wire, endless hours, seeing the sun sink and rise in the corner of her eye. Fighting the bigger ones, the stronger ones; layer upon layer of scar tissue forming. *This is what we do with wild dogs, Key.* She was stronger now; useful.

"Yes, Commander, I benefited."

Lara left Jackie's office with a sense of unease settling deep in her gut; she'd have to do better from now on.

A voice beside her startled her out of her musings; surprise growing as she beheld Roman.

"Hello, Lara."

"Deputy Commissioner."

The older woman huffed. "You Bound lot, such sticklers for formality."

Lara's only response was a tight smile. Her cheeks ached with the strain.

"I've been meaning to thank you, Lara, for bringing those pamphlets to our attention. We've been worried about those liberationists for a while now; you've given us just what we needed."

Her chest was tight, the realisation settling in; she must have disappointed Roman too. Lara swallowed – she'd accept the consequences.

"I apologise, ma'am."

"Oh." Roman looked nonplussed. "For what?"

"For how I acted at the time; for losing control like that. It was unbecoming of me."

Silence prevailed, and when Lara finally looked up

she was greeted with a gaze so soft she flinched. Roman's voice was hushed.

"I had thought yours and Jackie's experiences to be the same, but they weren't, were they? No one's ever are."

"I'm sorry?"

The deputy commissioner moved forward, Lara falling into her leader's heady atmosphere.

"Not everyone's made to be a Greycoat, you know."

Lara blinked, willing Roman's face to sharpen from the haze that had settled across her vision.

"In Bound we're made to do as we're told."

Suddenly a warm hand landed on her shoulder, pleasure coiling though her veins like living tendrils.

"Then I'm telling you, Lara, it's OK to be wild."

She wandered away from Roman in a serpentine manner, everything heavy and hazy and far too pleasant for the last dredges of winter. Before she knew it she was before Hadren, stood by the kennels with a wide smile. Her partner cackled loud and long.

"I see someone's been talking with the DC."

Lara grinned lazily. "How can you tell?"

"You've the look. I mean, you could have just come; it's a similar look."

"How d'you know I didn't come with Roman?"

Hadren gave her a playful shove. "Bite your tongue."

They laughed, the world slowly coming back to Lara in sharpening clarity.

"All there now?"

"Yes. How does she do that – is it magic?"

"Uh, I assume so. Roman has a way with living things, it's just..."

"No one knows what way."

"Exactly."

Lara frowned, taking in their surroundings. "What were you doing in the kennels?"

"I wasn't in the kennels."

"But–"

"Let's go." Hadren was off, Lara trailing after her in confusion.

When she finally caught up the other woman was looking dead ahead.

"We're off to see the Steam Syndicate. They've had a break-in."

The Steam Syndicate – she'd read about them; pored over articles each and every day. They always seemed to be in the paper for some reason or another, although she wasn't sure some of those reasons were really newsworthy. What did anyone care what Watterson Teach was wearing?

"Have you ever met any of the Steam Syndicate, Hadren?"

"I knew Ash Sevo a little. The Ajartan community here is pretty tight knit; my parents knew his."

"Not friends, then."

"Barely even acquaintances. And for all the inches I read about Teach and Cinnabar, I've never actually seen them in person. Evie was a few years above me in school so I know her a little." Hadren paused, bumping her shoulder into Lara. "I guess this is a first we can share." Lara's heart warmed; she was glad to have Hadren.

The syndicate headquarters were blander than she'd imagined; just a big, square brick building amongst a host of big, square brick buildings. Yet from the open windows she could hear the sound of machines clanging and rattling, and shouting drifting out on the breeze. A man in a sharp red-and-silver uniform stood by the door, squinting as they approached.

Lara took centre stage. “We’re here to speak with Cinnabar and Teach regarding a reported break-in.”

The man ducked inside wordlessly, an abrupt shout of “Leon!” startling them both.

Beside her, Hadren snorted. “Proper Cerranites, this lot.”

The man reappeared, gesturing them through without a word.

Lara was struck by a wall of heat, thick and cloying and smelling of labour. Burning caught her nostrils, sparks flying and flames flickering all about. Such chaos put her at ease. There was laughter and cursing from all angles, and in the corner of her eye she spotted Andromeda conversing with a man with skin like burnt caramel and waves of thick, dark hair heavily flecked with silver.

Lara pushed down the urge to go to her, instead walking on with her companion. Eventually they came to a woman with oil up her arms, sharp, dark eyes and a wide nose smudged with soot. She nodded at their approach.

“Good morning, I’m Leon Tsaika.” Lara didn’t recognise the accent, but it was nice, wispy. She wondered if this Leon could sing.

“I’m Constable Gogh, this is Constable Key. We’re here about the break-in you reported.”

“Oh right, Modesto has the list of everything stolen. I’ll take you up to him.” She paused before moving off, glancing shrewdly at Lara. “Have I seen you before?”

"Not that I'm aware of."

Leon shrugged and moved on, taking the steps two at a time, long legs climbing effortlessly as the young cadets trailed after her. Lara chanced a look back, seeing Andromeda still fully immersed in whatever the handsome man was saying.

They stopped so abruptly she almost walked into Leon's back; glancing over their guide's shoulder, Lara frowned. There was a young boy sat at the desk, head barely reaching the top of his chair. He'd thick black curls, skin just a tad lighter than Hadren's and arms like twigs. Lara saw though, despite being half hidden by that desk, the clumsy puppy possibility in those limbs, just waiting to grow.

She could hear Leon's frown as she spoke. "Wes, why aren't you in school?"

He shrugged. "I'm spending time with Mods instead." Wes glanced across the office, a tall man emerging from another door. Lara liked his freckles – and his scowl.

"These officers are here to talk you about the break-in, Modesto."

He said nothing, gently nudging Wes with a bandaged hand.

"Go with Leon and find Watt."

Wes nodded, springing out of the room with a merry farewell, Leon going to follow but pausing beside Lara.

"You've a fantastic right hook, Constable Key."

Lara watched her go in confusion, shrugging at Hadren's look of curiosity.

When Lara looked back at Modesto he was still scowling, although it appeared more like habit than general spite.

Hadren cleared her throat. "I'm Constable Gogh, this is Constable Key. Tsaika said you have a list of what was stolen."

"I do."

A silence followed, Lara's hands twitching with the awkwardness of it all. Finally she spoke. "May we see it?"

He pulled a slip of paper from the desk, glancing at it briefly before handing it over. When he came close enough Lara smelt cinnamon and, just underneath, rubbing alcohol.

"Thank you."

"It's an odd list." His voice was rumbling and rough, singing through her brain. "I'm not sure what their aim is."

"So you've no idea what they're planning to make?" She liked the green in his eyes, dark and deep and lovely.

He looked straight at her as he answered. "It depends on what they already have." Paper crinkled to her right; she'd almost forgotten Hadren was there.

"They could be selling for scrap."

Modesto shook his head. "I don't think so. None of that fetches much."

"Well, we'll see what we can find."

"All right. Thank you." He didn't sound overly enthused, sinking down into his chair without another word. Lara cast a glance back as she followed Hadren out, trying in vain to get another glimpse of those green eyes.

Chapter 12

INTENT

The sunshine in the puddles made Ridley wince, so bright and clear it was like all of Cerrano was a star. She squinted out of the doorway, freshness in the air and the scent of rain still lingering in the merry sunshine. She'd lain awake all night listening to the storm batter the tower, thunder rumbling through her veins as lightning flashed against the windows. Something about it kept her alert, muscles wired in anticipation. Yet the morning had only brought the sun and a vibrant blue sky, nothing to be concerned about. Friday appeared at her elbow, looking fresh-faced as she linked their hands together.

"Let's go for a walk."

"All right, Friday." A larger hand squeezed hers, the two of them wandering off into the damp, sun-drenched city.

Their footsteps rippled the puddles, Ridley watching as the water danced in celebration as Cerrano thrummed with life. Her skin warmed in the sunbeams, blasting the last remnants of winter from her bones. She looked to Friday, delighting in the light casting her features so coppery.

"Are we going anywhere in particular?"

"The Rise, perhaps? We can see which gods they deigned most worthy of attention."

Ridley nodded. "Want to take the streetcar?"

"No." Friday smiled brightly, swinging their joined hands as they walked. "It's so nice out, let's take our time."

A few glanced their way as they went on, but Ridley's mood was too content to be bothered by it, merely letting the stares slide off her like water off steel.

Friday cleared her throat. "So, I've been thinking."

"A dangerous game indeed." She bumped their shoulders, marvelling at Friday's mirth.

"Very funny. But in all seriousness, I've made a plan."

"Oh, we're being serious?"

Friday let out a sigh, smile betraying her despondent words. "I see you're in no mood for proper conversation today. I'll just save my plans for a guild till another day."

"A guild?"

"No, no. You're obviously not interested, which means you're not invited to join either."

Ridley laughed at Friday's pout, leaning up to peck at her cheek.

"Don't you try and sway me, Shadow."

The pleasing, peaceful morning was soon drowned in noise, Ridley tightening her grip as they came across a large crowd. At the head two women were speaking, and Ridley's scowl darkened as she looked on.

"Friday, it's her."

"I know." The taller woman pulled her along. "Let's go." Ridley couldn't tear her eyes away, still feeling the stranger's breath on her face as she leant in. Whoever she was, the crowd were enthralled.

"We come here, not in anger or indignation, but in peaceful unity. We ask only for the same as those magical; the same respect, the same opportunities. For what are our differences really? Beneath the skin, down in the marrow, are we not the same?"

Each word drew cheers from the crowd, a mixture of genuine optimism and jeering dismissal. Ridley could practically smell the tension rising, as magical and not jostled for a place. Friday huffed as they shouldered their way through.

"We best go home."

"This won't end well, will it?"

As if summoned by her words, the Greycoats arrived, circling the crowd like sharks. Their appearance ignited the unrest, the two women still onstage calling for quiet.

"We've no quarrel with the Greycoats today, we're simply here to speak. Our cause has no intent for violence." The other woman had her hands held up, placating despite the firmness of her tone. "You aren't needed today."

Suddenly Ridley was pushed into Friday, stumbling as the crowd surged.

"We will decide when we are needed, Evie Teach."

Through the bodies she saw a Greycoat, tall and blonde, well adorned with medals across her breast. She'd a face of steel, the throng parting in desperation as she moved forward. "You and Shoshanna have made no declaration of your intent to speak here today. This mob has gathered illegally. Now disperse, or you will be moved."

So the stranger had a name: Shoshanna. Shoshanna and Evie Teach. Ridley kept her eyes on the crowd, wary of locking with those abrasive eyes.

"Any violence brought forth today will be of your making, Commander King. We are peaceful, but we will not be silenced."

The crowd began to murmur, Ridley catching suspicious glances thrown her way.

"Enough of this shit." Friday gripped her hand tight enough to bruise, pushing unceremoniously through the spectators, barely moving before the commander's voice rang out once more.

"Very well." A whistle pierced the air, the mass of people surging anew as shouts and cries echoed all around.

Ridley shoved at a woman who made to grab her, dodging through the agitated mob till they broke through the edge, only to look up into the golden gaze she'd met before.

"Roman?" The grey of her uniform did nothing to diminish her; if anything Ridley thought her even lovelier just to spite it.

"I'd not taken you two for agitators."

Beside her, Friday bristled. "We were just out for a walk." Barking and shouts cut across them, Roman gesturing swiftly.

"Lara, escort these two out of the square, I don't want them caught up in it." The young blonde woman to her left nodded, barely curtailing her unabashed wonder as she looked at Ridley.

"Of course, Deputy Commissioner." Without another word Roman entered the crowd, the Shadow tracking her as people bowed out of her way. "Come on."

Lara led them away, hardly taking a few steps before the screaming started. Ridley froze.

"What are they doing?" The situation was descending rapidly, the Greycoats working their way through the crowd in ways she was glad she couldn't see. The barking grew as people fled.

"The dogs are trained properly; their handler won't let them really hurt anyone, I assure you." Ridley saw Lara's conviction in every line, but it didn't quell the pounding in her chest.

"This was completely unnecessary, they weren't hurting anyone."

Ridley leant in to Friday, grateful the other could say what she couldn't.

Lara wasn't swayed. "Maybe not yet."

No sooner had the words left the young woman's mouth than a great explosion ripped through the air. Friday's arm instantly curled over Ridley's head as a wave of noise and heat sent them stumbling. Her ears were ringing, the sounds of people and still-barking dogs gradually rising under the residual noise from the blast. She looked up just in time to see Lara running off, sprinting towards a huge plume of smoke as it danced into the sky.

Chapter 13

FIRE

Fire had a sound, a gentle, spitting crackle that signalled warmth and light. It was the sound of a small hearth, a chance to finally sit down by the little flames and rest a weary soul. The song of fire was pleasant, comforting, but that's not what Lara heard now. The inferno roared; that lovely little crackle had become something grotesque as the flames ate through the building, supports groaning and buckling as they turned to ash. Would she share the same fate, should the inferno engulf her? Would it gnaw her bones like those once-mighty wooden pillars?

"Lara!" That pretty face overtook her: Andromeda in all her glory standing between her and the blast's aftermath. "Lara, are you all right?"

Her mind shifted, the heat of the blaze a fog that stifled the shouts of others. Hands shook her shoulders, Andromeda's brow creased with worry. Lara wiped the sweat from her upper lip, casting her eyes about.

"Where's Hadren?"

"Who?"

"My partner." Through the chaos she caught a glimpse of Roman ushering people away from the perimeter and let out a wavering breath.

A dog bounded past her, fur mottled with soot. It was sniffing at the air, jumping and paws worrying the ground. Two more quickly followed suit, along with a man with long, dark hair, a cut bleeding sluggishly on his forehead; she couldn't smell the copper over the fire. Lara knew him, though, recognised him and his slightly altered uniform – the kennel master's apprentice.

"Dory?"

He swung back to her, dogs close on his heels.

"It is Dory, isn't it?"

"Yes."

"Have you seen Hadren – Cadet Gogh?"

"She's containing the blaze round the other side."

"She's all right?"

He nodded. "Luckily the building's been abandoned for months, but we need to get in and check."

As he moved away she steeled herself, muscles coiling and heart thumping. If they needed to get inside, then Lara would get them in.

"Wait."

She halted, turning to Andromeda with a scowl.

"Let me."

"This is Greycoat business, Andromeda."

The other woman scoffed. "It's Cerrano's business."

"You'll get hurt."

"Trust me, I won't." Without another word Andromeda

approached the building, stride unfaltering as she encroached on heat and flame.

A beam had fallen across the entryway, charred and blackened but still sturdy. Lara looked it over, the ceiling where it once hung already scattered about them. Sweat poured profusely, soaking her back and seeping through her clothes. Putting her hand on the beam she made to push, but her comrade's voice stopped her once again.

"Stop."

"It's not supporting anything, I'll knock it down."

"I know, but it might bring down something else. And the fire could jump."

Lara growled. "And you propose what, then?"

"Throw me." She must have misheard

"Excuse me?"

"Throw me. With your strength I'll knock it down."

"And break every bone in your fucking body."

Andromeda smiled, stepping into Lara's space and crowding her away from the flames. "I told you to trust me, Lara."

Being so close Lara couldn't help but steal a glance at those lips, finally noticing that no sweat hung above them. Andromeda wasn't sweating; not a single drop of perspiration on that pretty face.

"You're impervious?"

"I'm impervious."

"So…"

Andromeda leant back. "So throw me."

Lara's lip curled, halfway between a snarl and a smile. She gripped Andromeda's belt tightly, the other hand going to her collar. Lifting her effortlessly above her head, she took a deep breath, feeling the charred air creep into her lungs.

"Tuck in tight, Andromeda." With all her might she let loose, power thrumming through her limbs like a mighty current propelling the other woman into the flaming building. The crash sounded out into the sky, but Lara wasted no time to see anyone's reactions, bounding into the blaze just in time to see Andromeda stand, nonchalant in her dousing of an ignited sleeve. Indigo eyes met hers.

"Let's see who's to save, shall we?"

The flames licked at Lara's clothing, her chest tight as smoke invaded her lungs. She squinted into the building, Andromeda a shield beside her, and waded in.

"I don't think there's anyone in here."

Lara nodded, ears pricked to the continuing groans of swelling wood echoing around them.

"Let's get out. I need to tell Deputy Commissioner Ion." She turned to find the other woman kneeling, hands turning over something small and charred. "What's that?"

"I'm not sure. But I've seen it before–"

A sudden, ominous creaking pulled their eyes upwards. A large staircase was half-hanging through a hole in the ceiling, dangling over their heads.

In a burst of speed Lara shot forward, power lending her the strength to grab Andromeda as a harsh splitting filled the air. She didn't look back as the din smothered the sound of the flames, holding tightly enough to feel the bones creak in the other woman's hand as they stumbled through the debris. The walls screamed as the fire engulfed them, finally licking its way through the last of the structure's strength as Lara and Andromeda burst out of the blaze.

By the time the ringing had stopped Lara became highly aware of her position, lying on the cobbles with Andromeda draped over her back, warm and solid and safe. She took in a lungful of blessedly cooler air, chest expanding as her friend rolled to stand.

"Fire's out."

Lara blinked owlishly up at her, shifting just enough to see the now-decimated building billowing smoke from its mangled carcass.

"So it is."

She gingerly sat up, cobbles digging into her ruined uniform to gnaw at the heated flesh beneath. People were still yelling all around, the lack of wails or screams a marginal comfort. Perhaps there really wasn't anyone in there.

"I know where this came from." Looking back at Andromeda, she caught a flash of dirtied bronze, the small object tight in her hand, metal sizzling under flesh that would not give way.

"What is it?"

"A timer. One I recognise." Abruptly she stood, offering Lara a helping hand. "Follow me."

"I have to report in."

"Do that when you have something to report."

Lara faltered, eyeing the other Greycoats warily through the smoke. Perhaps she could make up for Market Town; perhaps she could impress Roman and Jackie. She looked to Andromeda, stood dirtied and steady, and nodded.

"Lead on."

Chapter 14

SINS OF THE MOTHER

The scent of smoke danced in through the open windows, Watt's nostrils flaring as he stared out at the distant, diminishing plumes. He kept reciting in his head, *Mods is at home, Wes is at home, Leon's downstairs, Evie's at the Rise.* Again and again the list ran through his mind, a stampede of worry keeping him at the window, eyes glued to the distant chaos. Each name was a shaky inhale, their whereabouts a chance to let it out. Breaths slow and measured lest they choke him on their way down. His hands trembled by his sides, heart refusing to calm as he fought despairingly against the panic burrowing into his chest. *Mods is at home, Wes is at home, Leon's downstairs, Evie's at the Rise...*

All was quiet below, the usual sounds of the factory silenced on a rare day off. Only Leon was about, no doubt believing it best to give him a wide berth. Over the litany in his head he could still hear her, footsteps climbing the stairs to his office – although it didn't sound like Leon. She was light on her feet, scaring the life out of him on more than one occasion. Whoever was coming to see him now wasn't quite so stealthy.

A figure appeared up the steps; it was Leon after all, although she wasn't alone. Andromeda hurried after her, followed by a young Greycoat who sent woefully familiar shivers of Jackie bloody King down his spine.

"Watt, Andromeda and Constable Key wish to speak with you."

"Constable Key?"

Leon gestured to her. "She came the day before yesterday. About the break-in."

"Oh, my apologies. You must have spoken with Modesto." Modesto, who was at home with Wes. Watt needed to see Evie.

"We did, he gave us a list of missing things. Which is what we've come to talk to you about."

As Key came closer he noticed the state of her: clothes charred and askew, hair even more so. She held herself well, though, he'd give her that; the grey lending children the courage to speak with the authority their years had yet to grant them. By Io Sola, Andromeda was only seventeen, and her blonde companion looked even younger.

"You were by the blast?"

They nodded, Andromeda moving to stand beside the officer.

"We saw Evie leading a protest. She wasn't caught up in the explosion." Finally the litany in his head quieted, heartbeat stuttering to a normal rhythm. "However, she has been arrested."

He sighed, long and weary. "What for this time? She was meant to be at the Rise."

"Inciting the people to violence and protesting in a non-designated area." Key stared resolutely at him. "And she was rude to Commander King."

"Of course she was."

He laid his head in his hands, neck suddenly too weak to support it. By Garrin, she grew more like her mother every day.

"Leon?"

"I'll take care of it, it was all for show, I'm sure." He heard her steps fade, reluctantly lifting his head to find Andromeda and her Greycoat staring at him expectantly. Frowning at their proximity, he clocked the easy way they were leaning towards each other, probably wholly unaware of the other's pull.

"I'd no idea you'd a pet Greycoat, Andromeda."

"She's not–"

"Lady Knight is assisting in official business. I am *not* her pet." Oh, he'd struck a nerve. Key was doing her utmost to remain passive, but he saw war dancing in those eyes. War, indignation and, if he'd thought himself the observant sort, pain.

"As you say, Officer." It didn't mollify her, but he found himself all the happier for it. He'd spent too long appeasing Greycoats when there were more important things to do – fuck being level-headed; they'd arrested his daughter again.

Andromeda held out something small and blackened, ash coating Watt's hand as he took it. He rubbed the soot with his thumb, revealing tarnished bronze and a small, ruined clock face beneath.

"We found it amongst the wreckage; I remembered seeing some here. Constable Key confirmed timers were on the list of stolen pieces Modesto gave her."

He turned the thing over in his hand; it was still warm. "That's right."

"With that in mind, do you think it likely that the items stolen from you were used to make an explosive?" Key didn't blink, staring straight at him with an unnervingly steady air.

"Likely? I couldn't say. But is it possible? Yes."

"Have you any idea who might have robbed you?"

It was Watt's turn to be stern. "I thought figuring that out was your job."

Key bristled, but Andromeda laid a gentle hand on her arm. He really shouldn't have been so welcoming that first time she appeared.

"Thank you, Watterson, we'll see what we can do about Evie. Won't we, Lara?"

"Of course, Ro… Deputy Commissioner Ion wouldn't keep someone who'd done nothing wrong."

Lara suited her better than Constable Key. Watt's indignation guttered and died under the open expression she gave him; a child again once her work was done. He took pity on her.

"I should probably say, we don't make these timers."

Lara cocked her head. "No?"

"No. Leon purchased them from the new inventor in the old clock tower. I think her name's Friday." He didn't mention the Shadow Shoshanna had met – who knew what trouble a casual mention of her could bring?

"Friday. That's great, thank you, Teach. For your time

and your help." Oh, she had a bright smile; he couldn't stop himself from returning it.

"That's quite all right, Lara Key. Andromeda, I suppose I'll see you tomorrow."

As their steps diminished he deflated, sinking onto his chair and relaxing every muscle. Barely midday and he was already exhausted. The Mother take this emotional whiplash.

Heavy, hurrying footsteps invaded his mental mire, and without looking up he called out, "Did you forget something?"

When no response came he cracked open an eyelid, standing abruptly once he beheld Modesto in the doorway.

"Mods?"

"I didn't know where you were."

Watt blinked, taking in his friend's flushed cheeks and heaving chest. "Did you run here?"

"The streetcar stopped after–"

"The blast." Quickly he made his way over, stopping in front of Modesto with a hopeful heart. "You and Wes are all right?"

"Yes, he's at home. Evie?"

"Fine. In prison again, but fine otherwise." He took a step forward, marvelling in their closeness. For a week Modesto had avoided him, ducking out of rooms and conversations the moment Watt appeared. But now here he was, breathless and worried and *here*.

"You were worried about me?"

"Don't be an idiot, Watt." He watched as Modesto fought down his smile, trying unsuccessfully to twist it into a grimace. "Just because we haven't been speaking doesn't mean…"

"I'm sorry." It was instinctual, primal, this need to make amends. Having Modesto avoid him, be *frightened* of him, was too much to bear. "I've been trying to say it all week but…"

"I know."

"You do?"

"Yes, I know."

The smile that split Watt's face pulled painfully at his cheeks, relief and joy refusing to be tamped down. "Do you forgive me?"

Modesto nodded. "Yes, Watt, I forgive you."

Watt practically threw himself at the other man, arms tight about Modesto's waist and head tucked over his shoulder. He felt the other's arms come up around his neck, beard scratching his face and still smelling of cinnamon and iodine.

"You're a fool, Watterson Teach, but I forgive you anyway."

As they pulled away Watt righted himself, feeling more balanced than he had in weeks.

"So, should we go get your daughter from her newest cell?"

"No, Leon's gone. Let's just go home and wait for them, no point planning Evie's birthday if she spends it in a cell."

Modesto frowned. "Are you sure?"

"Yes." He thought of that bright smile, of Lara Key and Andromeda Knight, and felt more secure than he had since Ash was alive. "We've friends in the right places."

An incidental mention, that's all it had been; an off-the-cuff word of condolence from the governor.

"Terribly sorry about Evelyn; shame for a family like the Warrens to lose such a daughter."

He'd just sat there, mute, nodding along to her apologies. The syndicate's streetcar plans lay forgotten before him, foolproof pitch now only shards of an unsaid speech he'd crafted with Ash – Ash, whose hand landed softly upon his shoulder, who herded him out of there without a word. Suddenly it was just the two of them, safe in his parlour. Those hazel eyes shone up at him, like gold peeking through moss.

"Hey, you with me?"

And he was, reality crashing down around him. Evelyn was dead, slain in some far-off field, no doubt dying for victory; it was just how she would have wanted it.

"She's dead, Ash."

"Yeah, yeah, I know."

"They didn't even tell me." It hit him hard – Evelyn's family had never liked him; too ordinary for a Warren. "Oh, gods."

"What?"

"The Warrens – what if they come for Evie?"

Ash moved to sit next to him, sofa creaking. "Why would they?"

"Why? They just lost a daughter is why, they'll want a replacement."

The burst of laughter shook him, Ash's sense of humour wringing the grief from his bones.

"What's so funny?"

"I'm sorry, but are we talking about the same Evie?"

Watt bristled. "What's that supposed to mean?"

"Watt, look, I love Evie. You know I do. But the girl has about as much magical talent as Modesto."

The knot in his chest lessened, anxiety abating in the face of Ash's compassionate clarity.

"She's not even five yet."

"You know it doesn't take that long to show up."

Acceptance settled in, Watt leaning back and letting the familiar weight of it wash over him. He'd tell Evie about Evelyn, not that she'd understand enough to grieve; how could she mourn someone she'd never met? By Fortella, how could he, when he hadn't even missed her – had barely liked her?

"Speaking of Modesto…"

He straightened, eyebrow rising at the seriousness on Ash's face. "Were we?"

"Don't think this is some sort of excuse…"

By the Mother, not this again. "Excuse for what exactly?"

"For fucking him."

"I beg your pardon?" Heat crawled up Watt's spine, and he cursed the ease with which Ash riled him up.

"You heard me."

"Ash Marty Sevo, the mother of my child just died."

"As if you care."

Watt glared hard, guilt struggling to take hold under his skin.

"Watt, come on. I hated her, she and Mods hated each other, and you can deny it all you like but you did too."

"She's dead."

"That doesn't change how she lived. You two had an awful not-relationship for barely a year, and you didn't speak till just before the birth, purely because that's when she told you. You barely spoke at the birth and then a day

later she left. That's it. What are you meant to be mourning here? The image of Evelyn you kept in your head?"

He grumbled, loath to admit just how right Ash was. Surely the dead deserved to be mourned.

"If you feel the need to grieve for someone that never really existed then fine, but for Mamarra's sake don't get maudlin just for the sake of it."

Had he spoken out loud? No, Ash just knew sometimes; it'd be astounding if it weren't so annoying.

He sighed. "All right, fine. But I didn't hate her, or I haven't for a few years at least. Evelyn was who she was – a lot of people respected her for it, I just… took some time to realise that. She doesn't need my grief; she wouldn't have wanted it anyway."

Ash nodded, looking far too pleased with himself.

"However, that doesn't mean I'm going to start jumping into bed with the next pretty thing that comes my way."

"You think he's pretty."

"Gods, I walked right into that."

"And besides, he's hardly a 'next thing', Watt, he's Modesto – and what do you mean, 'start to'? You sleep around plenty."

"Don't be jealous."

"I'm not – hey, we're talking about Modesto here."

"Why exactly are we talking about him?"

The look Ash gave him could have cut glass. "Watt, you've wanted him long enough for us both to be a little uncomfortable about it. Just because he hasn't noticed doesn't mean no one else has."

"It hasn't been that long."

"Regardless," Ash held up a hand, levelling Watt with

his most fearsome gaze, "he's not another notch on your poor, poor bedpost. Touch him and I'll break your hands."

Watt sunk down into his chair, hands tucked protectively under his armpits. "You're meant to be my friend."

"Oh, Watt, I am. This is what's best for both of you. Now, let's go find Evie."

"Don't sound quite so upbeat at the prospect of telling my daughter her mother's dead, Ash."

"It's my natural setting."

Watt grumbled as Ash pulled him to standing, slinging an arm around his neck.

"Yes, I suppose it is."

Chapter 15
WHITE TEETH

All the world was muffled and soft, heavy blanket a cloud-shaped shield around her, trapping in the blessed dark. Ridley burrowed deeper into the cushions, downy softness gentle and kind. Through the layers the faintest traces of Friday's singing managed to penetrate down, soothing her back to sleep. Yesterday's catastrophe had leached the energy from her bones, leaving them feeling hollow and fragile. Even now, after sleeping so long and so deeply, the dull, aching emptiness lingered at her centre. She needed to get up, but the very thought atrophied her limbs. Friday wanted her up too, that gentle singing a reminder of her continued presence; she could get up for Friday.

Ridley pushed a hand out, the bedroom air only slightly cooler than her body-heated tomb, but her skin tingled all the same. With a huff she pulled herself along after, blinking at the dimmed room. Through a small gap she saw the light of day fighting its way through the heavy curtains to bathe the room in a dreamy, reddish glow. Specks of dust floated in the air, atmosphere just as sleepy as she. The humming petered out, a soft chuckle taking its place.

Friday was at the mirror, Ridley catching those storm-cloud eyes in the glass.

"Morning, girl, welcome to the land of the living."

"If this bed is Io Sola, then I've no idea why we've held death off so long."

Friday hummed fondly. "The usual, I suppose. Vengeance, grief, impossible promises…"

"Oh, that's right." Ridley glanced up as the bed dipped, Friday's hand moving to tangle with the knots atop her head.

"Will you be getting dressed today, Shadow, dear? Only I've a guest coming over."

"Guest?"

"From the Steam Syndicate."

"Oh, the Orysh girl." With a groan Ridley pushed herself up, body protesting and difficult as she moved to their bathroom.

"Will you be joining us, then?"

She mulled it over as the sink filled, the cascading sound echoing in the little room. "I'd rather not get involved."

"I know." The coolness of the water slapped her skin, pores tingling her into wakefulness. "Leon's not so bad, though, you might even like her."

Friday was back at the vanity, half-dressed and pulling a brush lazily through her hair. Ridley tracked the movement, breathing in time with the strokes.

"Me liking her isn't really the problem."

The brush stilled, and Friday's voice was strained as she spoke. "If Leon does become a problem, it's not one you'll need to worry about."

"All right." *I'd rather you didn't either* hung between them, the words too heavy and clumsy for her tongue to shape. She watched Friday go with a sick feeling; things went wrong so quickly.

An hour later Ridley made slow progress out to the workshop, the steady, perfectly timed song of the gears spurring her on. The weight of her hair pulled at her scalp, skin too tight across her bones; she should have stayed in bed. Her space was empty, but from the front merry chatter floated back. Friday's laugh hit her ears, and the hollowness in her chest began to fill.

The grin sent her way upon turning into their sight was all she needed; a flash of white teeth brighter than the sun.

"Ridley, this is Leon Tsaika. Leon, this is Ridley Ripley."

Leon's teeth were shining white too, a little sharper-looking – though no one had more bite than Friday. Her eyes were as black as her hair, pupils invisible; the edges crinkled when she smiled. It was quite sweet really.

"Morning." Ridley moved forward leisurely, arcing around Leon to settle on the other side. Friday quirked a brow.

"Leon's from the Steam Syndicate."

"I remember, you told me this morning."

"Will you be joining the guild also?"

"Guild?"

"The one Friday and I are setting up. You're an inventor too, aren't you? You built all this?" Leon gestured about her, at the clocks and the toys, nuts and bolts fitted together in perfect harmony. She hadn't meant to include the tower in her grand gesture of course, but Ridley startled for a moment all the same.

"I did, yes."

"So you'll join?" Leon smiled her satisfaction, and Ridley turned a questioning gaze to Friday.

"I didn't know you were serious about this."

"This city's full of inventors, it's high time we got together. Made sure our interests are taken care of."

Before Ridley could process her lover's words, footsteps sounded from below, signalling the arrival of two young women, one of whom she recognised. Friday stepped forward as Lara and her companion came into the shop, shoulder in front of Ridley. Her tone could cut glass.

"Can we help you?"

A soft chuckle came from behind, Leon moving in amongst the situation. "Don't worry, Friday, it's just Lara and Andromeda."

Despite the assurances Ridley felt the cold close in, the aforementioned Andromeda's eyes glued to her the second she'd entered. That indigo intensity ran straight through her bones, turning her legs to stone. Their voices drifted away as the world became awash in shades of purple till a familiar growl cut through the haze.

"The fuck are you staring at, haven't you ever seen a Shadow before?"

Andromeda faltered, clearly caught off guard at Friday's intensity. "No, my apologies…"

"Don't apologise to me."

Lara cut across them, gaze trained solely on Friday. "We're not here to argue with you. We've simply come to ask some questions about yesterday's incident."

"What about it? We only saw as much as you."

"It's not about the incident itself so much as the device used. It was constructed using a particular timer that you make." The officer pulled something small from her pocket, holding it out for Friday, who, unmoved, simply stared. "Could you please–"

"I know what it is. Yes, we make those. Besides Leon here, no one else has purchased any."

"You've had no break-ins?"

"No."

"I see. Well, thank you for your time."

They turned to leave, but Friday, who was obviously in a mood, called out after them.

"Oh, Andromeda?"

"Yes?" The young woman stopped, glancing between everyone except Ridley with tremulous eyes. It was amazing in its own way, the ease with which Friday could knock you off kilter. Even if they'd never seen her in action she exuded something intrinsically intimidating that people couldn't help but cower from. When they'd first met, battlefield before them, Ridley had only guessed at the capacity for damage Friday could unleash. Although, it'd be hypocritical of her to judge.

"Why are you here? This fine officer of the law I understand, but you – what business is this of yours?"

Leon's gentle murmur of "Friday" went unacknowledged as Lara went in, shielding Andromeda in much the same way Friday did for her.

"Lady Knight is a member of the Citadel, assisting me on official business."

"And do politicians often escort officers on their duties, or are you particularly concerned for your safety in this tower?" They were nearly nose to nose, the inches Friday had on Lara doing nothing to dissuade the Greycoat.

"What exactly are you insinuating?"

Ridley watched Friday's snarl, Lara's eyes level with her teeth. "I'm not insinuating anything, little girl. I'm telling you I know *just* what you're thinking. You should take more care in who you offend."

She was impressed; Lara held her ground better than most Ridley had seen. The trembling, though, could not be overlooked. The girl's skin seemed to be vibrating, fear and realisation rattling through her frame as she began to comprehend the woman before her. Ridley had been that girl once.

"Friday." All eyes snapped to her, shock, relief and curiosity alight in each. "It's fine, let them be."

Friday looked back to Lara. "It must be your lucky day, girl."

Chapter 16
A FRAGILE THING

Her cheek tingled, the feel of Andromeda's lips a shock that refused to dissipate. Lara watched her go with wide eyes, ears still ringing with the other's professed gratitude. Taking a deep, shuddering breath, her whole body relaxed, heart singing in some unknown rhythm. Once Andromeda was out of sight she turned through the grey gate, practically floating her way into the Highfort. All that fear Friday had left her with stolen away with a kiss; perhaps today wouldn't be so bad after all.

A familiar sound drifted into her consciousness, an invisible rope pulling her to stop before her partner.

"Hadren."

"Lara, why so merry?"

She let out a sigh, willing her happiness to spread out into the city. "I've just had a nice morning." A very nice morning, Friday's threat notwithstanding. Barking erupted nearby, and once again she realised where they were. “Hadren, why are you at the kennels again?”

“I’m not.”

“You’re clearly–”

“The commander wants to see you before we go on patrol.”

She gaped. “Why didn’t you say so straight away?” Swiftly turning, Lara bid a hasty farewell, glancing back only to see her friend peering round the kennel door. Lara shook her head, hurrying away from Hadren and her confusing quirks.

As she encroached on Jackie’s office her heart rate picked up, the familiar door a beacon of unease. What had she done now? Her knock was greeted with a brusque summons, to which she steeled herself and entered. To say Jackie looked bothered was an understatement; her top button undone and usually immaculate hair slightly out of style. She had a veritable swamp of papers on the desk before her, but they were soon forgotten when she locked eyes with Lara.

“Key.”

“Good afternoon, Commander, Cadet Gogh said you wanted to see me.”

“Indeed I do. Take a seat, Key.”

At times Jackie reminded her so much of Bound it made her sick. All that platinum posturing a glaring reminder of what she should be, of what awaited her should she fail.

“I find myself in awe, Key, that we’re having this conversation again.”

"Ma'am?"

"I've received word that you didn't report in to a senior officer after the blast, that you entered the building whilst it was still aflame without being instructed to, only to then leave it in ruins. You ran off with a non-Greycoat, who, I've been informed, you threw. Into. The building."

Lara's jaw clenched, teeth grinding as she bit down on her excuses. They were never welcome. Jackie had remained measured as she spoke, but her eyes penetrated Lara's in indignation.

"Do explain this to me, Key."

"Andromeda Knight is an envoy from the Citadel."

"You threw a Citadel official into a burning building?"

"Yes, ma'am. Though one impervious to harm."

"For Gallara's sake, why?"

"To get in."

Jackie leant back in her chair, shoulders so broad they touched each side. The creaking set Lara's eyes twitching.

"Under normal circumstances I'm sure there'd be something to be said for your zeal, Key. But you and I do not come from normal circumstances. We were shaped by a finely crafted system, one which chose our duty with care and finality. In anyone else your eagerness and enthusiasm would be commendable."

The last vestiges of warmth left by Andromeda's lips finally faded, leaving only the stinging frigidity of Jackie's barrage. Lara's hands were cold.

"However, you are only you, and as such all I can see is a legacy of Bound lacking in discipline."

After all these years the words still cut her deeply. She glanced up to find Jackie's face a hard, unforgiving mask.

"Do you know what happens to the undisciplined, Key?" *This is what happens to wild dogs, Key.* "What should happen to you, should we be forced to remove you from our ranks?"

Sweat was pooling on her lower back, stomach churning and heart thumping a parade. All the new recruits would watch the feral girl, test their mettle against the woman too undisciplined, too wild to serve Gallow as she ought. Bone upon bone shattered and reformed till she was a deceptively hardy thing, whiling away her days as an example to the young. *Follow your orders.*

"Do you understand, Lara?"

"Yes, Commander, I understand."

Chapter 17
FAMILY MANNERS

It was eating away at him, this constant worry. For over a month it'd been one thing after another that challenged his poor old heart; Watt was really feeling his age. Things were finally right with Modesto and now, rather than relaxing, he had new suspicions gnawing at his mind. It was Evie, Evie and Shoshanna and their grand plans for liberation. He'd tried so desperately to ignore the little voice in his head, the one that sounded distinctly like Evelyn, telling him over and over not to be so blind; to put the pieces together like he should, but Evelyn be damned, he didn't want to. Evie was more like her mother than he ever wanted to admit, so he wouldn't. Not even to the phantom ghost of her voice occupying his skull. *Perhaps I should speak with Modesto…*

As the resolution formed Evie came bounding down the stairs, hurrying past him with rolls of paper tucked under her arm. It was now or never.

"Happy birthday, Evie, are you staying for breakfast?"

She spun on her heel, hair flying everywhere. "Sorry, Dad, rally to get to. Organising to do, etc. etc. Thanks, though, I'll be back later, OK?"

"Oh, of course, I've got your present–"

"Tonight, Dad, tonight. Got to get going." She smiled brightly, his concern diminishing under her unbridled confidence. Moving back, she narrowly swerved Modesto, who had his own stack of papers to balance.

"Careful."

"Sorry, Mods, I'll see you later. Save me some dinner." She grabbed him by the neck and planted a noisy kiss on his cheek, hurrying off with Modesto's shout of "Happy birthday" trailing after her.

"I want a baby."

Watt stopped, pen poised an inch above a sketch he really wasn't enamoured with. He looked up to see Ash gazing longingly out of the window. Sounds of their gleaming new workshop filtered in through the office door, Evie's laughter dancing above it all. At his friend's despairing sigh he finally gave in – the blueprint was poor anyway.

"You want a baby?"

"Yes, do you think I'd make a good dad?"

"Without a doubt."

"Really?" The naked hope on Ash's face nearly blinded him – where had all this come from?

"Of course, look at how you are with Evie."

Ash beamed, nodding happily before settling back to his work.

Watt frowned. "Was that it?"

"Pardon?"

"Crisis over?"

"Well, now I know I have your support..."

"Support for what?"

Ash squared his shoulders. "I'm going to the Temple of the Mother tomorrow."

"Oh, so you really *want a baby."*

"Imagine my features on a baby – how cute would that be?"

Watt chuckled. "It could look like the surrogate, you know, since you're going that route."

The younger man merely shrugged. "Either way, it'll be perfect."

After a few words of well-wishing Watt went back to his work, studiously ignoring the silence from the other desk. Apparently Ash wasn't quite done.

"What about Mods?"

Watt sighed; it looked as though designing a steamboat wasn't in his future. "What about him?"

"Do you think he'll come?"

"Where, to the temple?"

"Yeah."

"He doesn't want a baby, Ash. Ever, as far as I'm aware."

"Well, I know that; besides, he's only a baby himself."

"He's twenty-three next week."

"He's a baby. Anyway, if he did have one, it'd take his attention away from you and we can't have that..."

"What?" Shit, the way Ash was looking at him only meant one thing: he knew. Watt sniffed, brushing it off. "You're talking shit."

"I know you fucked him."

Watt froze, tongue leaden in his mouth.

"He told me."

"Like fuck he did."

"Aha! So you did have sex."

Watt's head hit the desk, the sensation doing nothing to dull the irritation dancing through his veins. "For fuck's sake."

"It was mid-autumn, right, before the feast? I knew you two were acting shifty."

"Ash, please, for the love of–"

"Come over here."

"Why?"

"So I can break your hands."

Watt scowled, staring resolutely down at his work. "He could've seduced me, you know."

Ash snorted. "Oh please, Modesto Cinnabar couldn't seduce someone if his life depended on it."

"You don't know him as well as you think you do."

Ash took great offence to that, if the look he sent Watt was any indication. For a moment he looked so annoyed it seemed as though he'd go back to work, but, as Watt had seen many times over their long friendship, curiosity got the better of him.

"So, are you two together now then?"

Sometimes Watt wondered if his closest, oldest friend was sent to Eera merely to test him. Likke was the god of puzzles and lies and truth; perhaps he should pray to her a bit more.

"No, Ash; at least, we've not discussed it."

"But if you did discuss it, maybe–"

"Maybe nothing, after that shitshow yesterday."

Gods, yesterday, he'd be lucky to get anywhere near Modesto after that screaming match.

Ash frowned. "But I'm the one who shouted at him."

"Yes, but I didn't exactly defend him, did I? I agreed with you."

"Of course you did, he was being reckless. There's a reason only magics make flying machines."

"I know, and he does too. But my intentions don't mean much to him right now."

Ash hummed, calculations whirling through that brilliant brain, trying to make some sense of things.

"D'you think he'll still come to the temple?"

Watt couldn't stop the warm smile from taking over his face. "Of course he will, he'll do anything you ask of him. So long as you ask nicely."

"If it's lentils again we're getting a new cook."

Watt looked to his friend, mind sluggish to comprehend anything but his own thoughts. "What?"

"For dinner. I assume he's doing Evie's favourite, but..." Modesto frowned, tilting his head as he observed the older man. "Are you all right?"

"I think it's pie."

The younger man smiled, Watt watching in awe as his whole face lit up.

"Firing all guns this morning, I see."

"You've a lovely smile."

"Thank you, but don't try to distract me."

"A bit of flattery now and then never goes amiss."

"Not if it's sincere, no."

"With you, Modesto, I'm always sincere."

"Could you possibly not be such a horrendous fucking flirt for one moment?"

In a fit of fancy Watt grabbed at Modesto, pulling him in and spinning him in a whirl of fallen papers.

"Watterson!"

"Yes, dearest?"

Modesto pushed him away, desperately trying to force a grimace over his smile. "You can pick those up."

Watt saw him go with a laugh, joy drowning out his earlier worries.

"I just wanted a dance."

His knees creaked as he knelt. Groaning loudly, he began picking up his friend's plans. As he shuffled them a worryingly familiar shape caught his eye, appearing again and again in only slightly varied forms. This was just what he needed on top of everything else: Modesto on a veritable suicide mission. Gathering everything, he proceeded into the office, finding the other man with his back to him, staring out at the mansion's heart garden.

Watt gazed beyond the glass to all the exotic plants, brightly coloured and beautiful. Light from the fading day still tumbled in from the great glass skylight; a backdrop lighting Modesto's outline like some holy creature.

"Have you been taking care of the garden?"

Modesto jumped, turning to see him with the sun at his back.

"Uh, no. Wes and Leon have taken it upon themselves; I think it helps Wes feel closer to Ash."

"I suppose it would."

Painful though it was to cut through the peace, the

plans in his hands could not be ignored. Steeling himself for the argument to come, he put them down.

"Modesto?"

Said man arched an auburn brow. "Watt?"

"Why are you designing this again?"

With a puzzled frown Modesto looked down, and Watt saw the moment clarity tensed the other's shoulders.

"We agreed–"

"You and Ash telling me no is not *we* agreeing to anything. It's you." Modesto's nostrils were flaring, his eyes fixed firmly on his desk; he must have known this talk was coming. "What gives you the right to look through my things anyway?"

"You dropped them all over the floor."

"Because you made me." With a grunt Modesto dropped into his chair, pouting like a petulant child. At least now Watt knew where Wes learned it.

"If you didn't want me to see them why didn't you pick them up?"

The younger man shrugged. "I forgot I was carrying them."

Watt perched on the desk, careful not to disturb any of the myriad things his companion had littered it with.

"Mods, you promised us you'd let this go."

"I know. But an airship builder from Kadeja Heights asked me and I–"

"Who?" There were dozens of airship builders down in that city, all of them clamouring to distinguish themselves in some way. Though which one would be desperate enough to design a craft without magic was beyond Watt.

"Primrose Karl."

"Of *the* Karls?"

"Well, I don't know of any others."

Watt shook his head. "Look, Mods, I understand your desire to do this, but with everything else going on right now I think dangerous designs can wait."

"What is the syndicate for if not this? Not just the enhancement of the non-magical, but the freeing of those magical from the path they are bound by? Just because Primrose Karl can make something fly doesn't mean she wants to all her life."

"I know."

"And why shouldn't the likes of you or me or Wes make something soar purely because we want it to?"

The yearning in Modesto's face was enough to make Watt pause, but then flashes of Ash's coffin came back, of Evie's face covered in building debris fresh from the Highfort cells. He stood to his full height, leaning over his friend with a hand bracketed on either side of the other's head. The chair creaked as he intruded, Modesto shifting to sit back in vain.

"Leave it, Modesto. I'm telling you, I cannot bury anyone else."

The other man let out a breath, slouching back down in his chair. "All right."

Reluctant to accept such an easy victory, but more so to keep fighting, Watt smiled. Leaving a brief kiss on Modesto's forehead, he leant back, muscles in his back protesting.

"What other things?"

He blinked down, those green eyes piercing right through him. "Pardon?"

"What other things are going on? Andromeda doesn't seem eager to get us in trouble, and we've dealt with our safety issues. So what other things are causing you such grief?"

He could've lied, could've fled; but Modesto had been honest. It was his turn.

"I'm worried Evie is the one who stole from us."

"To what end?" The disbelief was clear in Modesto's voice, his affection for Evie equal only to Watt's own. Loath as he was to ruin it, he needed another opinion.

"The end to which Lara Key alluded."

"You think Evie set that fucking bomb?" Modesto was up and pacing in an instant, fists clenched and expression dark. "She'd never do something like that, Watt. Cunting Bayona, I don't know where your head goes these days."

"I'd be inclined to agree, but I've been privy to conversations you haven't. Conversations about attention and anger, told to me by an increasingly angry woman."

Modesto stopped, weighed down with sorrow.

"Evie wouldn't hurt anyone."

"Not intentionally..."

"Not at all."

Watt steadied himself, hating the words before he'd even said them.

"Are you forgetting who was really in charge of safety at the factory?"

If Modesto had looked sad before, he seemed shattered now, falling back into his chair in abject despair.

"I thought you weren't going to tell her."

"I didn't, Mods. But that doesn't mean she hasn't figured it out. Evie's not stupid."

"No, she isn't."

"It wouldn't take much for her to realise she killed Ash."

Chapter 18

THE SHADOW

There was fur on Hadren's sleeve, a few loose, golden strands just above her cuff; innocuous and incriminating all at once. Lara squinted at them, head throbbing with sudden understanding.

"Are you fucking Dory Apiece?"

Sputtering and a pair of wide eyes answered her as Hadren tried to contain herself. "What?"

Lara smirked, appraising her partner anew and registering the blush under her dark skin. "It could be the kennel master of course, but I'm fairly certain it's not considering her less than stellar people skills."

"Bit rich coming from you."

Lara shook off the insult like it was nothing, skin far too thick for such lazy jibes. "So are you, then?"

"Am I what?"

"Fucking. Dory."

Hadren frowned, nostrils flaring in what Lara couldn't decipher as rage or fear. "Yes."

"He seems nice."

She turned back to her food, chewing robotically as Hadren stared at her, dumbfounded. Jackie's words had kept her up all night; images of a life left to rot in Bound a tumult in her head. The food couldn't quiet it, Hadren's indignant mutterings faded beneath it, and all the sounds of Cerrano were nothing more than a metronome for the painful pounding behind her temples. Not even the fleeting thought of Andromeda stood a chance against her maudlin mood. If only she'd just done as she was asked. The porridge was heavy on her tongue, bland and unwanted; she couldn't take any more.

A shadow fell across her. Craning her head, Lara once again found herself in Jackie King's unwavering gaze.

"Key, Gogh, once you've finished here I'd like you both to report to my office." Without waiting for, or likely expecting a reply, the commander left. Lara stared forlornly into the middle distance, packing up her memories of this place with her meagre belongings.

"Gods, you're in there more than King herself. Does she not like you or something?" Hadren's questioning gaze was given with a smile, humour falling flat against Lara's current mood.

"No, Hads, I don't think she does."

As the commander's door came into sight her chest tightened, only Hadren's warm, steady presence keeping her throat from closing. Gods, what awaited her beyond that door this time? Was Hadren there to watch her dismissal, finally promised to a better, more reliable partner; no more to be bound to the wild dog of Bound?

All noise was lost to the erratic pulsing in her veins, mind screaming at her to take a deep breath; to just breathe. Hadren moved in slow motion, knocking on the door with a casual motion, pushing it open languidly. Lara felt sick – by the Mother, this was it. They stepped in, Jackie gazing at them from her seat. Bile was creeping its way up Lara's throat, but then she saw a flash of gold.

"Good morning." Roman was perched on the windowsill in a languid recline, lazy smile in place. All at once Lara felt loose in her limbs, tension and fear bleeding out of her under that kindly gaze.

"Good morning, Deputy Commissioner Ion." Hadren's voice boomed loud in her ear, her own relief clogging up her throat when she attempted to reply. Roman had told her it was OK to be wild; she wouldn't let Jackie send her away. A jab in her back signalled the room's impatience, the three of them staring at her in confused silence.

"Good morning, ma'am."

Roman shuddered. "Oh, don't call me ma'am, Lara. Makes me feel old." How that voice tugged at her heartstrings.

Jackie cleared her throat, and Lara reluctantly forced her eyes away from Roman.

"Deputy Commissioner Ion and I have been discussing the witness accounts from the blast, and one person has been mentioned as present more than any other." A grunt to her left was met with a frown from the commander, but she continued despite Roman's guttural interruption. "The Shadow from the clock tower was reported by multiple witnesses to have been seen supporting suspicious behaviour."

Lara bit down on her own interjection; proper soldiers didn't offer opinions.

"And despite Deputy Commissioner Ion's assurances, High Commissioner Stone believes it prudent that the Shadow be interviewed–"

"Ridley Ripley. Her name is Ridley Ripley, Jackie."

Even when aggravated Roman sounded more pleasing than all the trainers in Bound, although Lara felt her irritation deeply. She watched, rapt, as Jackie schooled her features back to their stern indifference.

"I've also been informed, Key, that you and Ripley have met before."

Lara fought down the worry – how could they know? Perhaps Friday had put in a complaint, or Tsaika?

"As such, we assumed you to be on slightly better footing with her."

Wait, what? They'd hardly parted on good terms… *oh.* They meant at the rally, when Roman had introduced them.

"Yes, Commander."

"Right, then you and Gogh will interview her today. See what the Shadow has to say."

With a brusque dismissal they turned to go, Roman's melodious tenor holding them in place.

"I want you both to be courteous, do you understand?" Roman stood, closing in on them as the sound of Jackie shuffling papers quieted in the background. "Ridley Ripley deserves as much respect as, and perhaps more kindness than, everyone else. She is, at least to my mind, the victim of a memorable face. I trust I don't need to tell you the cruelty of that?"

Lara murmured a low "No, ma'am", hearing Hadren do the same.

Jackie sighed. "Roman."

Said woman's eyes were intense as she stared at them, something desperate and unfathomable in their gilded depths.

The commander cut through their moment. "Gogh, Key, you have your orders. Go speak with the Shadow."

Chapter 19

SCARS OF HARLEON

She liked copper, liked the sheen and the shine and the smell. Liked how it reminded her of Friday; the burnished colour so like her hair and freckles. It was tough, too, just like her. Not the strongest of metals, easily shaped, easily damaged, but it wouldn't break. Just like Friday when they'd first met all those centuries before. When the Shadows had said no it was Friday who convinced them, convinced Ridley to lend their aid. There was an innocence to that steadfastness then, an earnest, hungry belief to it, but that was long ago. Copper had turned to magma, burning and volatile – and it'd been all her own doing.

A knocking sounded on the shop door, ripping Ridley from her thoughts. She grunted, running her fingers along a smooth copper ring as she called out, "We're closed."

"Constables Gogh and Key of the Cerrano Greycoats. We're come on official business, please open the door." Constable Key – Lara. Had that girl no survival instincts?

"All right." Leaving her work in a mess she pushed herself up, throwing out a prayer to whoever that Friday would not return before they left.

There was Lara, standing behind another officer, eyes so wide they were practically screaming at her.

"Good morning, are you Ridley Ripley?"

Well, she'd not heard her name said quite so casually in a long time. In fact, Roman Ion had been the only one to say it at all; even Tsaika hadn't called her by name, and she'd been in her company more than enough. Now here was this officer, hazel eyes all bright in her ebony face, addressing Ridley as though she were anyone else.

"Yes."

"We've come to ask you a few questions about the blast that occurred on the 27th of last month."

Ridley frowned, flicking her gaze to Lara, who remained silent and wide-eyed.

"You want to speak to me again?"

The girl stiffened, wincing near imperceptibly. Oh, someone wasn't playing by the rules. Constable Gogh gave her a disarming smile.

"I'm afraid so. The accounts we gathered at the time of the blast were just to gather the basic information. Which we're now following up."

"I see, come in."

She leant against a workbench, watching them move into the room. Lara, bless her, still looked tight as a bow; tension made Ridley uncomfortable.

"Constable Key, was it?" Lara's eyes were so brilliantly grey, just a shade down from white, nothing like Friday's tempestuous storm clouds.

"It was."

"I believe we've met once before, at the rally. Only briefly, mind." It was like she'd popped a balloon, all the tension in that girl bleeding to leave a relived puddle on the floor.

"Yes, Deputy Commissioner Ion asked me to escort you to safety."

"A valiant effort it was, too."

Without those unspoken worries in the air the atmosphere in the room shifted and Ridley breathed freely again. The other officer, Gogh, looked between the two of them with a thoughtful eye, but there was no maliciousness that she could see. Clearing her throat, Gogh stepped forward.

"We've had numerous eye witnesses that put you in the area at the time of the blast. Did you happen to see or notice anything suspicious?"

Ridley's heart sunk – even with the air of nonchalance Gogh couldn't hide the meaning behind her questions. The aching exhaustion crept its way up her spine as memories of old questions and questioners rose to the surface. Some of them smiled, called her by her name, even: "What did you see, Ripley?" didn't take long to become "Tell us the fucking truth, Shadow." Gallow never changed.

"Suspicious?"

"Yes, anyone of less than reputable repute?"

"I've only been here two months, I'm not sure who the malcontents are. You saw me." She turned to Lara, who'd remained silent for a while. "I'd only have seen the same as you and Roman." The girl nodded but didn't speak, hands clenching convulsively at her sides. "The only ones causing a commotion were the two onstage."

Something crossed Lara's face, her hands stilling. "Evie Teach and Shoshanna."

"Is that their names?" The young woman seemed gone, though, lost in her own head, Ridley turned back to Gogh. "I'm sorry I can't be of more help."

"No, you have been." The officer looked uncomfortable now, and Ridley groaned internally. The woman had obviously been hoping for a slip-up, for her to reveal something in rushed explanations or hollow excuses. Now she'd have to be direct; Ridley hadn't the stomach for arguments with strangers, but her indignation was beginning to grow.

"Was there something else, Officer?"

"I'm afraid as so many of our reports placed you at the scene–"

"Of course they did."

Gogh's mouth snapped shut, and she stared at Ridley with obvious intrigue. She'd not the time to sate it, however; Friday would be back any minute and she needed time to level herself. She couldn't greet Friday in skin that felt two sizes too small.

"I've a memorable face, Constable Gogh. A man on fire could run circles around me, and I'd still be the one they stared at. The one they accused of setting him alight."

"Sorry to have troubled you." Ridley swivelled to Lara, who was staring at her resolutely. It didn't make her veins hum any less. "It won't happen again. Thank you for your time."

Gogh looked pleasantly surprised as Lara beckoned

her to go, expecting to leave Ridley to her peace. Perhaps it would have been enough to lessen the weight on her chest, or stop her skin from scraping across her nerves, but then footsteps sounded below, and her heart stuttered in her chest.

"Damn."

Friday didn't notice them at first, her eyes trained happily on Ridley, but the second she did was obvious. All those ugly, violent emotions came out to play in full force on her face, beautiful mouth a vicious snarl. She rounded on the officers quicker than they could register her presence, Lara no doubt frozen with familiar fear.

"What is this?"

"We're here on–"

"I couldn't give a shit. Get out, you come round here again and I'll show you something far more terrifying than a Shadow."

"You can't just threaten officers of Cerrano."

As Friday stepped forward, so did Ridley, grabbing her lover's sleeve as the taller woman crowded into the officers' space.

"It's unwise for the likes of you to tell me what to do, *Constable.*" The word was said with the level of disdain Ridley had only ever heard lobbed at herself, and to hear it come from Friday ignited a fire in her belly.

"Friday, for fuck's sake, they're children. Leave them alone."

Suddenly Friday had hold of her, hands tight across her upper arms. Ridley gestured to the Greycoats to go, thanking every god there was that they did. Fingers squeezed tighter, the grind of bones and warmth of blood blooming purple beneath skin realigning her focus. She pulled, vicelike grip remaining tight.

"Let go, Friday."

"What in Io Sola is wrong with you?"

"What?"

"You were talking to the fucking Greycoats."

She yanked herself from Friday's grip, tingling replacing the encroaching numbness in her arms.

"We were having a conversation. One that'd come to a peaceful end before you stormed in."

"You shouldn't have been talking to them at all."

"Oh, do forgive me, Friday. I forget you're the only human I'm allowed to converse with."

"Don't give me that shit. It's not fucking safe, Ridley." There it was: the fuel to make her fire an inferno.

"Not safe? Not fucking safe? You think me such a monster I can't control myself for one second without you there?"

"Do not – don't fucking be like that. Don't raise your hackles at me."

But she couldn't help herself; it'd been so long since she'd let her anger out. So what if she knew what Friday really meant? She wanted violence, she wanted to hurt – and if she couldn't hurt herself…

"No, Friday, I think this is the perfect time. This fair city has decided your pet monster is a fucking arsonist now as well."

"What?"

"They took one look at me, one, and declared me the cause of all their troubles. The despicable thing in the clock tower coming down to set them all aflame."

"Then they're idiots–"

"But they're not, are they?" She'd lowered her voice, watching Friday struggle to rein herself in, bits of metal shaking and dancing through the air around them. "I *am* the thing they're scared of, the nightmare from the north they were warned about as children. How do the stories go again?" The speed of the flying debris increased, huge beams above them humming as Friday stared her down.

"Going into this hurts you more than me–"

"I recall my favourite, do you?"

"Fucking–"

"What was it called? You should know best of all."

"I said stop."

"Or should we go back to Harleon and refresh your memory?"

"What I did, I did for you."

"You made my people monsters. *The Song of the Shadows* is a fucking insult to their memory–"

"Enough!"

Hundreds of sharp thuds filled the air, the walls around them studded with all the shrapnel that had been dancing.

"You can be such a cruel cunt when you're afraid, Ridley." Friday turned away from her, leaving the Shadow with a crippling hollowness in her chest.

"I'm not afraid."

"You're always afraid."

Chapter 20
DEFENDER

Evie Teach and Shoshanna. It was clear to her now, now Ridley Ripley had inadvertently pointed the way. Evie Teach and Shoshanna had set the bomb. They had the means to steal from the syndicate, parts and plans and whatever expertise they wanted. Motivation was a little harder to grasp – what good such a violent commotion could lend their cause Lara didn't know, but she'd find out. Or at least, she wanted to. Hadren shot her down the second she'd said a thing. Lying in bed, Lara thought back to her partner's words, so resolute, so sure in their dismissal. *It was magic, Lara, only magic could have done something like that.* She'd have mentioned the irony of Hadren, of all people, being so dismissive if it weren't for the fact that she was to blame.

All their misguided suspicions, tracking someone like Ridley, all because Lara couldn't leave things alone. She turned that cursed timer over in her hands, metal regaining its shine as her fingers continued to smooth it round and round. She'd gone and taken the only piece of proof tying the explosion to the non-magicals, and now she couldn't give it back.

"Fucking Io Sola." Her hand flopped to smack loudly onto her chest. She'd fucked things up royally now; there was no way they could overlook what she'd done. She was done in Cerrano, finished. Unless…

"I find new evidence." That was it. Somehow, Lara would find something tying Evie and Shoshanna to it; they were guilty after all. She was sure of it.

Lara was shaken from her schemes as a great boom cut through the night, the force of the sound rattling the Highfort. From her window she saw nothing, quickly grabbing her jacket and flying into the corridor. Everyone was streaming out of their rooms, orders filling the air and ushering down into the courtyard.

"Key," Jackie caught her eye, speaking quickly, "you're with Apiece – accompany him to the incident." Without another word the commander left, issuing orders left and right.

Lara spotted Dory by the gates, four dogs by his side.

"Dory, I'm with you."

Together they and their canine cohorts made their way into the city, hurrying through crowds of civilians without a second glance.

"Do you know where Hadren is?" She watched the flash of surprise come and go; it was no time for explanations.

"She was sent ahead to contain the blaze."

"Was it another bomb?"

He nodded. "In the theatre district."

She sucked in a breath; the Shadow lived in the theatre district. As the clock tower, intact and noble, came into view, she let out a sigh. Surely Ridley would be left alone this time.

Her thoughts soon tripped, however, as she took in the inferno before them. It was twice the size of the last, the heat hitting her back when all she could see were the tallest flames licking the sky. As the smoke stung her eyes she moved by instinct, helping Dory and his dogs keep everyone back, allowing the officers to do their jobs. Briefly she caught sight of Hadren, arms moving in an intricate dance as she wrestled with the flames. As the heat and fire slowly died more people arrived to take in the spectacle; one in particular catching Lara's eye.

Lara moved towards the small group, Shoshanna standing before them gesticulating animatedly. Eventually she got close to enough to hear.

"Saw it prowling about. The Greycoats know and did nothing, so busy punishing us for anything and everything they let a monster like that roam our city." *Oh no.* "I say we go pay it a visit ourselves."

"What's going on here?" So engrossed was Lara that she'd not noticed Dory come to a stop next to her.

Shoshanna turned wide eyes to them, the picture of concerned citizenship. "Oh, Officers. We were just concerned that someone had been hurt."

Lara held back her snort, instead affecting her best air of Jackie. "I can assure you, Shoshanna, that we are doing all we can to minimise casualties and assist those in need."

The path of Shoshanna's eyes left an unsettling itch

across her skin, and when the woman blinked long and slow she had to refrain from lunging at her.

"Thank you, I feel safer already, Constable Key."

A growling filled her ears, and for a moment Lara thought it'd come from her, only to look down and see one of Dory's dogs baring its teeth.

"Please go back to your homes, this area is unsafe for the time being. Come, Manda." This Dory directed at the still-growling dog, which reluctantly moved away with Lara.

"I don't trust that woman."

Dory raised a brow, throwing an unconcerned glance back at the gathering. "Shoshanna? She's harmless, the more even-tempered if anything."

"More even-tempered than Evie?"

Before he could answer a flurry of activity began before them, Hadren appearing from the burnt-out carcass of a building and heading straight for Jackie.

"Damn." Lara glanced at Dory, whose face had fallen. "There are bodies."

Looking back to Jackie, she could see the straining of her shoulders, face as impassive as she could possibly manage. A niggling in the back of her head made her turn, and with a sinking feeling she watched Shoshanna and her group leave.

"Dory, something's going to happen."

He shrugged, gaze firmly on Hadren. "We've more important things to worry about."

She couldn't fault him, but Lara also couldn't shake the feeling broiling in the pit of her stomach. As their figures diminished it grew till, as her gaze travelled upward, the nausea peaked. The clock tower rose in the distance, and Shoshanna and her mob headed straight for it. *Shit.*

Without a word she slipped away, the others too preoccupied to notice her go. She hurried as fast as she could, dread trebling as she reached the tower, door wide open. Voices echoed loud and bitter down the stairs, covering her careful steps as she ascended. It came into view quickly, moonlight streaming in and illuminating the backs of a horde of people, all shifting and shouting in anger.

"Was you, fucking freak Shadow…–"

"Burning us all alive…–"

"Monster, that's what you are."

She'd heard enough, bounding into the room with thundering steps, not stopping till she'd placed herself firmly between the horde and the Shadow. She felt Ridley's eyes boring into her back, but Lara wasn't afraid of her. However, Shoshanna was nowhere in sight.

"All of you are trespassing, you will all leave at once." If the situation weren't so dire she'd have congratulated herself on her tone, but as it was she'd settle for the horrified looks on their faces. She realised Ridley hadn't said a thing, even when they were hurling abuse her way.

"You!" *Him again.* She'd fought that big man before; apparently it was time for another lesson.

"You will address me as Constable Key or not at all. Now, I will not ask you again; leave."

"Should have known, Greycunts got a fucking monster in their pocket." She heard Ridley shift, a few of the mob backing away; perhaps this wouldn't be so hard. "We'll leave when it's paid for what it's done."

His words echoed in her head, seething anger zeroing in on his red-tinted face. All those times of being treated like less, being called 'dog' or 'beast' or 'it' came swirling back to her till she was awash in fifteen years of tamped-down indignation and self-loathing. So Ridley knew how that felt? Well, Lara wouldn't let them get away with it. Her muscles tightened; she'd show this man what wild dogs could do. Moving forward, they stepped back, leaving her room to circle round them, fists preparing to fly. How she'd been itching for a fight…

A sudden force struck her in the back of the head, a resounding crack that rattled down her spine and sent her to her knees. Lara grunted, spots dancing in her vision for a second before the force came down again across her shoulders, wood splintering against the toughness of her bones even as her skin split. Vaguely, beyond the piercing pain, she heard shouting, a sudden flash of red darted by to her left, but as she turned a boot met her face, and all was dark.

Chapter 21

THE WEIGHT OF A BODY

Lara's blood was warm as it slithered down Ridley's neck, coming to pool in the dips of her collarbones, tepid and sticky as it cooled. She grunted, shifting the girl higher on her back, careful not to disturb the makeshift bandage of bedsheets across those damaged shoulders. Hot, moist breaths fanned out rhythmically across the skin of her throat, that young heart a steady, hardy beat against her back. Lara was alive, that was all that mattered, and by the Mother, Ridley would keep it that way.

Her muscles still twitched with residual magic, violent energy lingering in her limbs and the corner of her mind. She'd killed him, that man with the red face and the hateful eyes. She'd seen Lara go down and snapped; her temper finally reaching its end. The image of him slithered through her head, skin charred and bubbling as he crashed to the floor; innards as molten as the flames they'd witnessed. It hadn't been meant for him, it was that bitch she'd wanted to burn, the one who'd snuck up on Lara and walloped her so hard her shoulder blades peeked through the fragile, scarred skin of her back. That man had just gotten in the way. She shivered; losing control like that, in front of those people – they'd never forget. She'd be the monster till their dying day, no matter how many battered bodies she carried back home.

Lara gave a whimper, a small, pained sound that went straight to Ridley's withered old heart. She tightened her grip, hurrying towards the Highfort.

"Not long now, sparks; you're almost home." Gods, what would Friday say if she saw her now? Ridley shivered again for a whole new reason; Friday wouldn't be pleased.

Gradually, legs shaking from the effort, Ridley staggered into the Highfort, the light of dawn bright upon Lara across her back. It took an embarrassingly long time for the one officer on duty to look past her Shadow features and realise just whose head of crimson-spattered platinum was lolling on her shoulder.

"I could use some help." Her voice was significantly steadier than her legs, but Ridley suspected that might not last long. Not with the looks they were giving her and the metallic tang of blood clinging to her nostrils. Gods, why did she come here? Why did Lara fucking Key have to involve herself? The mob would have just done their damage and left...

"Ridley?"

Roman Ion, bathed in the sweet light of the newly risen sun and looking like some golden god; she was beginning to understand why people were always so enamoured with the woman.

"What happened – is that Lara?" Roman rushed forward, gently prying tacky strands of hair from the unconscious girl's face. As the older Greycoat's hand brushed her neck a wave pulsed through Ridley's body, knees one step from buckling. *Interesting.* "Come on, bring her inside."

With Roman's hand on her elbow a burst of strength propelled Ridley forward, tired body pulling what it needed from that gentle touch.

"Put her here." With the deputy commissioner's help she deposited Lara on a small bed, medics milling round her at once. With the weight and the comforting hand now gone Ridley was bereft, tiredness aching though her bones like an unwelcome song. All the blood that had dribbled onto her skin and soaked through her shirt had cooled, chilled and itchy and so very red.

"Ridley, what happened?" Roman was staring at her, voice firm but not unkind.

"Some people came to my tower, they said it was my fault. That I needed to answer for their loss."

"Their loss?"

"I don't know. They were too busy screaming and yelling to explain themselves clearly."

"And Lara?" Ridley watched Roman's concerned gaze go to the girl, eyes shimmering.

Her voice was half hysterical when she spoke. "She stepped in between us. Tried to… tried to defend *me.*" She tripped over the words, tongue old and clumsy with such foreign syllables. Someone had defended her, not Friday and her wrath, but a young girl too foolhardy to know better. Who looked at Ridley like something – someone – worth protecting.

"You're surprised." Roman gazed at her so intently, as if all her secrets were etched into the scars on her skin, hidden in plain sight, just waiting for the right pair of eyes. "You needn't be, it's what we do. It's what we're supposed to do." This last part she said softly, just loud enough for the two of them; like some shameful secret.

Roman blinked, looking Ridley over anew. "Are you hurt?"

"What? Oh, no. It's not mine."

"Where's Friday?"

It was like a kick to the chest, all the air going out of her in one harsh, scraping breath.

"She's out. At a friend's."

"Would you like me to have someone fetch her?" So much it hurt, but she couldn't. By the Mother, Friday was going to be so angry.

"No, best not. Friday wouldn't take kindly to being *fetched*. But, Roman, I–"

Just as she'd finally found the words – *I killed a man, burnt up his insides till his skin sizzled* – Commander King appeared at Roman's elbow.

"Deputy Commissioner, a word. We believe we've made an identification." The harsh grating of Jackie's eyes tore at Ridley's already frayed nerves; she looked so like Lara, but there was none of the girl's joy in Commander King. The woman gave her a pointed look as Roman sighed, turning back to Ridley.

"Sorry, Ridley, could you give us a moment?"

She couldn't, not now, her courage wouldn't hold.

"I can't, I'm sorry. I can't wait."

Roman frowned, not in anger or irritation, but she was clearly confused and, possibly, a little weary.

"What is it?"

"The people who attacked me, I'd fully intended to... I wasn't trying..."

Jackie was scowling even as Roman remained patiently waiting; though her expression soon turned to one of worry.

"Ridley, whatever happened, you saved Lara. We'll understand."

Jackie startled. "Lara?"

"She's all right now, Jackie." Roman turned back to Ridley. "Go on."

All the headway she'd made; Lara and Roman and even Tsaika. It was all ruined now, she always ruined everything. They'd have to start again, after Friday was finally finding her place... perhaps she could do what was best for both of them. Let them lock away the monster, and all would be well.

"I killed one of them."

Chapter 22

DAWN

"Are you sure you don't want to go home? Check everything's all right?"

She didn't turn around, though Watt didn't expect her to. Friday was… interesting, to say the least. When Leon had introduced them the day before he'd been wary of her, especially when he found out she was the growling guard in Shoshanna's tale. Yet they'd talked, and she'd been so interested in what he'd been doing, been so encouraging of them, that he started to think maybe Shoshanna had just met her on a bad day. Evie would like Friday, if only he could introduce them, but she'd been even more aloof than usual recently.

"No. I can see that bloody tower from here; it's fine."

He looked up as she grunted, turning to him with a deep scowl. She was an emotive sort, prone to frowning or face-splitting smiles, from what he had gathered over the course of the night. Damn Harlons; passionate and sad and secretive all their lives. Modesto was just the same, not that Watt had any idea what either of them had to be so sad about. Perhaps he could ask this Friday, maybe she knew what that cursed city was meant to be mourning. Mods certainly didn't… or he did. He'd always had a way with secrets.

Watt took a deep swig of his drink, the whisky burning down his throat. Friday nodded as he offered her the bottle.

"There's no shame in wanting to know. If it'd been anywhere near the mansion I'd have run there as fast as these old legs could take me."

He winced as she took a long pull, face showing not a single sign of discomfort.

"You're not that old. And she's fine."

"I'm sure she is."

He took another draught, deeper than the first, let it burn all the way down as he started at her.

"You're looking at me very intently, Teach, is there something you want?"

"Have you met Modesto?"

Her nostrils flared, a gleam of whisky shining on her lip. "Modesto?"

"My… my partner. Modesto Cinnabar, I must have mentioned him."

"Cinnabar's a Harlon name."

"He came down here when he was thirteen."

"I see. I'm afraid our paths haven't crossed, but then I've not been to Harleon in a very long time."

Watt looked down at his glass, watching the way the

lamplight filtered through the tumbler in fractals that broke the liquid's surface.

"He's a lot like you."

She quirked a brow. "Ginger?"

"Yes. Not just that, though; sort of angry too."

"You think I'm angry?" That brow of hers arched higher, but he felt no fear. He may have been drunker than he'd realised.

"Passionate then, but…"

"But…?"

"Sad. Like there's a maudlin edge to all his happy moments."

She smiled then, with that familiar morose curve; resignation that the bad things in life weren't to be avoided.

"You don't know me that well, Teach."

"No. But I know him; I know what to look for."

She tilted back in her chair, face showing no sign of that earlier maelstrom of emotion.

"What, is it some big secret?"

"Have you asked your Modesto any of this?"

Watt shrugged. "Sort of. I get the feeling he isn't quite sure himself."

"He's only young though, isn't he?"

"He's thirty-seven."

Friday's smile was sharp and bright. "Practically a baby."

"Do *you* know?"

That smirk faded, eyes growing distant as they left his face.

"Yes. I know."

Footsteps rattled out in the workshop, the harried face of Constable Gogh appearing in his doorway. She was flushed, covered in what looked like soot and, if Watt had to guess, burn marks on her uniform.

"Constable, is something the matter?"

"Commissioner Stone sent me to escort you to the Highfort..." Her words trailed off upon glimpsing Friday, no doubt weighing up some protocol or another. "In fact, it's probably best you both come."

Friday stood abruptly, drops of whisky splashing Watt's fingers.

"Where's Ridley?"

"Just follow me, please. The deputy commissioner wants to speak with you both."

Watt's heart sunk – was Modesto in trouble? Or Evie? Had she gotten herself involved again? Or what if... no. He shook those thoughts from his head; there was only so much tragedy a man could take.

Beside him Friday was silent as they walked, shoulders tense and jaw set. All that happy camaraderie gone. He'd have told her that perhaps the Shadow was more trouble than she was worth, but then he thought of his own little family. Watt had never been a hypocrite, and it was obvious, to those who knew what to look for, that Friday loved her girl too much to leave her.

Wes, they'd called him; Wes Matta Sevo. The middle name was Ash's father's; Watt knew that man well enough to know how much it'd mean to him. Their surrogate had gone that morning, kind and professional but not interested in hanging around and meeting the baby. Legally he wasn't hers; Watt could understand the need to go. Modesto had found it odd – no matter how much Watt explained the near holy occupation of it all, of donors in general, the younger man still questioned.

"It's just, Wes was growing in Laura; shouldn't she want to see him just once?"

Watt turned to him. "I think it's easier for her this way. Laura's done it a few times, Mods. She knows the best way to go about it."

"Yeah, and it's not like your parents struggled to be rid of you–"

"Ash!" Watt fought down his anger, watching in dismay as Modesto seemed to shrink on himself.

"I'll go get Evie, she's probably off the walls by now."

As soon as the door swung shut he rounded on Ash, the man looking all the more guilty with that squirming, gurgling bundle in his arms.

"What the fuck, Ash, where in Io Sola did that come from?"

His friend sighed, slowly putting Wes in his basket, letting go but not pulling away.

"I'm sorry."

"Don't apologise to me."

"I don't know why I said it, I wasn't even angry. It just came out."

"Gods, I thought I was meant to be the insensitive one. You know how he is about his family."

Ash hung his head; any other time Watt might have laughed.

"When he gets back you make it right."

"I will, the first second he's here."

Watt snorted. "It's like I've four children sometimes."

"You think he'll cry as much as Evie?"

Watt paused, gears shifting in his head. "Oh, you mean Wes?"

Ash giggled, a ridiculous sound for such a big man to make, but he did it more often than not. "Who d'you think I meant, Modesto?"

"Well, for a minute..."

Their laughter was cut short as Evie came barrelling in, Modesto pulled along behind her.

"Where is he, can I see him?"

"Of course you can, sparks, come see Wes." Watt threw a pointed look at Ash, leaving his two friends behind as he ushered his daughter to the basket. "Careful now, we don't want to upset him."

Evie nodded eagerly, peering at the baby with wide eyes. He took a swift glance over his shoulder, tension sliding away as Ash pulled Modesto into a hug, nearly taking the younger man off his feet.

"He's so small."

Turning back, Watt gazed, enraptured, at the image of Wes and Evie.

"Babies are small, sparks – you were too, not that long ago."

She scrunched up her nose, a not-quite-frown ruined by her good mood; he knew just who taught her that expression.

"Can I play with him?"

"Not yet, he's a bit too small right now. He was only born yesterday, you know."

She hummed, running a finger over Wes' tiny knuckles. "Can I help look after him then?"

"You're his big sister, Evie, that'll be your job."

When they reached the Highfort that dreadful feeling came back with a vengeance; the Greycoats silent and swift in their motions as the rest of Cerrano yawned awake. Before it could overtake him completely Commissioner Stone was before them, and the pity of her gaze turned his blood cold.

"Teach, please follow me."

He glanced at Friday, who was in a heated, hushed argument with Roman. There was that, at least: if it'd been really awful, really devastating, then surely he'd have been sent to Roman. She was the one who did the hard jobs, the one who knew how to be kind.

"Teach, if you please?" Stone was a few paces away, big green eyes patient as he pulled himself away from that golden figure and her pleasing voice.

Neither of them spoke as they walked through the halls, his chest tight with terrible anticipation. Up ahead he spotted a familiar figure hunched in a chair.

"Modesto?"

Said man looked up, relief shining in those dark eyes. "Finally. Will you tell me why we're here now?"

"What, isn't this because of you?"

"Me? I was at home asleep." Watt didn't believe that for a second; there was no doubt that Modesto had been home, but sleeping he was not. The man barely slept any more, and despite his protestations passing out at his desk did not count.

Stone cleared her throat. "Please come inside, I'll explain."

In a small side room they both sat, the commissioner across from them with her hands clasped loosely before her. Watt's chest tightened again, heart beating hard as it constricted.

"As I'm sure you are aware, another blast went off earlier this evening."

"The whole bloody country's aware–"

"*Modesto.*" Watt smiled sheepishly at the commissioner, panic heightening at the forced gesture.

"It went off in the theatre district at approximately 1.20 this morning. When we managed to get into the building, we discovered some casualties."

It was as though the whole world shrank, tunnelling in to the commissioner's sombre face – it wasn't one of his. It couldn't be. It wasn't Roman speaking; it would have been Roman…

He stuttered out, "It's not… not Evie?"

"No, Evie's not been hurt."

He let out a rattling breath, whole body deflating till he was little more than an overanxious bag of bones. Beside him, Modesto began to grumble.

"Then what in Io Sola did you drag us here for?"

Stone frowned, dark eyes flashing with something that made Watt distinctly uncomfortable.

"I said she wasn't hurt, I didn't say that she wasn't involved. Evie has been arrested under suspicion of terrorism and murder–"

"What?" He shot up, glaring down at the fearsome woman as though he could take her on, pushing down that fear her uniform had always caused.

Stone looked distinctly unimpressed, leaning back in

her chair and giving them both a once-over. If it'd been anyone else… but no, that was it. If Roman had given them the news, she'd have been kind, offered some belief in their cries against Evie's imprisonment. Stone wouldn't be so understanding; Watt doubted she knew how.

"Tell me, Teach, and do be honest: can you truthfully say Evie's behaviour of late hasn't given you cause for concern? That some of her associations haven't worried you?"

Watt's lips pulled into a snarl, teeth clenching back words he knew he'd regret. Suddenly a warm hand slipped into his, bandages scratching against his skin.

"Evie was at the rally when the first bomb went off; Commander King's the one who arrested her. What proof do you have that she had anything to do with either blast?"

"I didn't say she was working alone, Cinnabar; Evie is part of a very large, very intricate liberationist network. One that has decided violence is their only way forward–"

"Then it seems to me you need to police a little better. Maybe if you weren't all so heavy-handed they'd never have resorted to–"

"That sounds an awful lot like sympathy for their cause, Cinnabar. Where were you tonight?"

A growl tore out of Watt's throat, ragged and raw with frustration.

"Is this an interview, Commissioner Stone? Only you've given us no forewarning that it is so. That being said, I'd appreciate it if you kept your unfounded accusations to yourself, and let us see my daughter."

With that same placid face Stone stood, her blank stare only serving to make Watt's blood foam in his veins.

"I'm afraid that's quite impossible. She and her accomplice are being interrogated as we speak."

"Accomplice? What accomplice?"

A smirk, not overly smug but enough, enough for Watt to clench his teeth so hard he nearly heard them crack.

"The Shadow of course."

Chapter 23
WAKE

By Gallara, she hurt; every inch of her, every badly-healed bone and nerve ending all singing out in untold pain. As the throbbing dimmed from its initial intensity the world crawled in to take its place. Bit by bit she registered it all: the softness beneath her cheek, the cutting smell of antiseptic and, above it all, a gentle song, little more than a hummed melody. She scrunched her eyes, the aching in her skull buzzing with anticipation; was there another boot on the other side of those fragile films of flesh? Tentatively she opened her eyes, light renewing the pounding with vigour, but she refused to return to the dark. Blinking a few times, her vision focused, only for a vague, dark shape to sharpen into Andromeda.

She was staring blankly into the distance, singing softly and looking more dishevelled than Lara had ever seen her. She'd have laughed if she wasn't so certain it'd be torture. With a voice sleep-heavy and laced with discomfort, Lara spoke.

"Andromeda."

A screech followed as her chair pushed back, eyes running along Lara with startled joy as hands hovered nervously, desperate to touch but not daring.

"You're awake."

"Unfortunately." Agony laced up her spine as she failed to shift her arms, muscles atrophied from lying still and forced to heal too soon. Ah, that was right: someone had whacked her with a plank. "Fuck."

"Quite. Don't try to move, you moron."

Lara grunted, her glare not quite so threatening when half-obscured by a pillow; the position was doing nothing for her ferocity.

"Do you know who hit you?"

"I have an idea." Fucking Shoshanna, it was her, it must have been. Ridley Ripley would know. "I'll need to check with Ripley first, is she all right?"

Andromeda did not have a good poker face, and judging by the twitching look, something bad had happened.

"What is it, is she hurt?"

"No, Ridley Ripley is fine. Or at least, as fine as she can be."

"What's that mean?"

"It means the Shadow has been arrested, Key."

Just what she needed: Jackie King and the anxiety she wrought on top of her blinding pain. Well, it wouldn't do – lying helpless in front of Andromeda was one thing, but sprawling on her stomach in the company of the commander was one humiliation too far. With gargantuan effort Lara got her hands under her, shoulders and back screaming at the work. Sweat dotted her forehead as she pushed herself up, each sinew and shard protesting at the fiery discomfort sitting up caused. Ignoring Andromeda's entreaties, she levered herself around, hands a dead weight in her lap and stiff muscles singing.

"What in Io Sola is wrong with you? Stop moving."

She gave Andromeda a strained smile before turning to the commander.

"Why has Ripley been arrested?"

"For murder. And arson, terrorism and conspiracy to bring down the government, if you must know."

Gods, how long had she been asleep for that to happen?

"I don't understand."

"She confessed to murdering a man in defence of you, Key. A man you'd previously had an altercation with."

The big one, with the red face – she didn't even know his name.

"Ripley was just protecting me. Wait – arson? Commander–"

"Key, she burnt that man from the inside out, turned his organs and bones molten till he was nothing but a smoking, bubbling husk. All in an instant. With power like that they've arrested her as the magical fuel for Evie Teach's bombs."

Lara clenched her fists, feeling the nails dig and fragile skin split.

"Evie's? They've linked Evie and Ridley to all this; don't they know who I was defending her from? What about that fucker Shoshanna?"

"Shoshanna?"

"Yes, she's the one who attacked me."

"Commander–" Shouting cut across her, and Jackie shot her a pointed look before hurrying off with a last order over her shoulder. "Under no circumstances are you to move from that bed, Key, do you understand? Do. Not. Move."

Her head was pounding anew, fractured information and hazy memories slotting together imperfectly. She needed answers.

"Andromeda, how long have I been asleep?"

"Just over three hours."

"The three longest fucking hours. What happened?"

"Look, they've no proof to accuse Ripley really. Roman's been completely against it all so once you tell them about the fight they'll let her go. She did save one of their own, after all."

Lara nodded, brain sloshing about her skull. Fucking Shoshanna was still about, probably plotting her next move with Evie.

"Wait, why have they only linked Ridley to Evie?"

Andromeda's hand was colder than hers, skin smoother and such a healthy shade compared to how bloodless Lara currently was. Those indigo eyes drew close, still as pretty as when she'd first seen them, even marred with sorrow.

"They found Evie sort of half-covered in debris; she's fine but she was going on about the blast and how it wasn't meant to happen. She's all but confessed."

"She's been arrested?" As impenetrable as Andromeda was, there was no mistaking her anguish. Ignoring the nerve-racking pain Lara pulled her closer until it was impossible to discern who the tremors belonged to. “I’ve had my suspicions, I won’t lie. She wasn’t alone in this, Andy, but Ridley Ripley was not her accomplice.”

Andromeda sighed against Lara’s neck, thumbs rubbing lightly over the grooves of her spine.

“No, they’ll figure that out fairly soon, I suspect. It’s just Evie’s been saying she was there to stop it. To disarm it. She said she was trying to stop them.”

Lara pulled back, fixing the other with a determined stare. “We need to talk to them.”

“Them?”

“Cinnabar and Teach.”

“I doubt they’re in the mood for a chat, Lara.”

“But what if Evie’s telling the truth, what if she was trying to stop it? It stands to reason then that the one instigating it would be the person closest to her.”

“But why would Evie change her mind now?”

“We need to find Shoshanna first. For all we know Cinnabar and Teach could be next–”

“You’re certain she did this? They’re friends.”

“Well, even if she didn’t we need to find her. Shoshanna might know who did it. Whichever it is, Teach is our best option right now.”

By the Mother, moving was excruciating, every last speck of her railing against the pounding in her head.

“Whoa, we’re not going now, Lara, you’re still hurt – *stop moving.*” Andromeda’s hands made no difference as she stood, the other scowling as Lara moved her aside. “Fuck. I forgot how strong you are.”

“Strong enough. Where are my shoes?”

“Lara, the skin across your back is still knitting together–”

"What use are healers if they don't finish the job?"

"Don't be obtuse, it doesn't suit you. Just wait another hour or so."

"We don't have time, Andy."

"Fine, here." She handed her some fresh clothes, looking as though she begrudged every moment. "Hadren brought them while you were out. She wanted to stay but they needed her on duty."

Lara changed as quickly as her battered body would allow, sighing at the softness of the fabric against her damaged skin; she'd thank Hadren later. As they turned to go more shouting rang through the halls, the buckle of Lara's belt rattling. *Oh.*

"Is Friday here?"

"She's rather upset."

"Always upset, that one." Cracking her neck, Lara slunk past the busy officers, Andromeda a steady presence close at her elbow. Every step shuddered up her spine, sinking into bruises in full bloom and making her legs quake.

By the time they reached the syndicate HQ she was about ready to give, heart pounding wildly and skin itching all over. Healing was exhausting.

"We can take a break, you look like you're about to faint."

She shook her head, the buzzing behind her eyes picking up.

"No, let's go. You're sure they're in there? They didn't go home?"

"They're here."

Even through the fog Lara could hear the yelling and crashing, quieter pleas drowned out by another's rage. They paused on the threshold, watching the scene unfold. Modesto was stood on the ground floor, staring up at Watterson, who, with impassioned yelling, was tearing machinery up above and flinging it away.

"Watt, please–"

"What's the fucking point? None of it'll last now; they'll just take pieces till there's nothing left of us. Burn it all. What the fuck do I want with it?"

Modesto narrowly avoided another piece of shrapnel, somehow looking more battered than Lara felt.

"Watt, stop, just come down–"

In a fit of rage Watt tore an entire engine from its brackets, sending it careening towards Modesto, who stumbled over another bit of debris as he tried to dodge it.

Lara's knees gave out as she moved to cover him, adrenaline spent and body at its limit. As though in slow motion she watched through tired eyes as Andromeda calmly crouched in front of Modesto, not a grunt or curse escaping her as the engine collided solidly with her back. Shards and parts exploded against her in a shower of metal, yet she remained an unflinching shield above the stunned man. Their appearance must have snapped Watterson from his berserk mindset, as he let out an almighty yell.

"Modesto? Mods, are you all right? By Garrin, I'm sorry – fuck. Fuck. I didn't see, I'm sorry."

Gradually Lara reached them, stumbling to a halt as Watterson ran his hands along his silent friend. Tear-tracks on his face and blood on his hands, Teach was a mess.

"Mods, please? I'm sorry, I'm so sorry."

Modesto blinked, bleary gaze drifting over Lara, Andromeda, the engine debris and, finally, Watt's devastated face. He twitched his broken hand, letting out a quiet hiss.

"Modesto?"

"It's all right."

A raggedly pained sob tore from the older man's throat as he clutched Modesto to him, apologies and what sounded like nonsense tumbling into the other's skin. Lara looked to Andromeda, questions and sorrow clear in her gaze. They were intruding, but if they hadn't, well, Teach would have potentially been saying farewell to more than just Evie.

"We need to ask you about Evie." Andromeda's voice was gentle, enough to let the men know they were still there without cutting the atmosphere; Lara knew she'd never pull that off. Modesto met her eyes over Teach's shoulder, the pain in them clear.

"We should get you to a healer."

As Watt pulled back he nodded at Lara's words, careful as he helped Modesto stand.

"I'm fine–"

"You're not."

The men shared a look Lara didn't want to decipher, Watt's hand shaking on the other man's arm.

"Please, Modesto." A small nod was his only reply, but Watt let out a watery sigh as he slipped a hand around Modesto's shoulders. Andromeda came suddenly to Lara's side, arm about her waist.

"You too."

"Me?"

"Yes, you – think I didn't notice you fall? Or the fact you feel like a furnace?"

"Forced healing will do that."

"Overexertion will do that too. Healer, now."

Slowly the four of them left, hobbling along as fast as they were able. Eventually Teach broke the silence.

"I assume you didn't come just to save us from ourselves?"

"Not quite."

"The joys of parenthood are truly endless."

Through the pounding in her temples Lara picked her words carefully, tact wavering like her consciousness. "I don't think Evie set those bombs alone. Or at all."

"Nor do I."

Lara froze, hearing Modesto's noise of protest as Teach hushed him.

"I wasn't sure before, but… but I know now."

"Can you prove it?"

Andromeda's fingers dug into her hip bone, cutting though the haze.

"Not yet, but someone else can."

"Shoshanna?"

Teach's eyes darkened, teeth flashing at the mention of her name. "Yes. They planned things together, and whatever went wrong between them, that cunt is going to tell us all of it."

Chapter 24

PERPETUAL GRIEF

It was better to let things heal at their own pace, they said, to give it time. Forcing something that had been forced before, that was still fragile, was liable to make it worse. Besides, they weren't confident Modesto had the energy to spare. Staring at that freshly bandaged hand, Watt considered the possibility that maybe he didn't either. That initial burst of agony and rage had faded so swiftly, burned out to leave him raw and hollow. The world without Ash was finally starting to right itself, only for it to violently shift again. A world without Evie wasn't a thing he planned to witness.

Modesto jolted beside him, the battle to stay awake coming to its inevitable conclusion. Watt wound his arm round the other's neck, pulling him in till their sides touched.

"You can sleep a little if you want, Mods, the healer said you should."

"I'll sleep once we're home. What's Andromeda doing? I thought she was just making sure Lara was settled and checking on Evie."

Watt sighed as the younger man relaxed into him, watching the Greycoats move with weary indifference. "Maybe something went wrong. Lara didn't look particularly well, did she?" His only answer was Modesto's head coming to rest on his shoulder, hair catching his beard. "I'll wake you once she's back."

"I'm just resting my eyes."

"If you say so."

"I am. If I sleep now I don't think I'll be able to walk back."

"Then I'll just have to carry you."

"You can't, I'm bigger…"

"In your dreams, Modesto."

Despite his objections Watt felt Modesto's breath slowly even out, the steady rise and fall of those shoulders under his arm all the company he could handle. He tried to focus on it, on the hustle around them, but his mind refused to remain blank. All he could see was her face, his Evie, shipped off to Princetown to disappear with the worst Gallow had to offer.

It was Evelyn all over again; violent ends for those who loved so violently. Evie was a soldier in her own way, a commander of legions just like her mother, though she had always seemed to lack Evelyn's steely disposition. She'd do badly in Princetown, a person with no magic in a place like that… Was it Evelyn's bloodied footsteps she was following or some cosmic balance for what had befallen Ash? She hadn't meant to kill him, but then, if Watt's suspicions were true, she hadn't meant to kill anyone. Could this have been an accident? Could Shoshanna…?

"There's been a fire."

Watt blinked, mind sluggishly shaking off the haze of sleep, barely registering the words. Commander – no, Deputy Commissioner Ion was stood on his doorstep, glowing in the lamplight of just before dawn.

"A fire?"

"I'm afraid so. It's engulfed half of your workshop."

Oh, damn – who would break in and do something like that?

"I see, just let me wake Modesto and Ash."

"Watterson…"

He froze; the pleasing undercurrent he'd come to know in her voice jolted hideously on his name, other things trying to force themselves up through the syllables. His heart beat thunderously against his chest.

"Watterson, I'm sorry, but Ash was inside."

"What?" He couldn't have heard right, he couldn't have. He was still asleep, only half aware; Roman wasn't saying…

"I'm so sorry, Watterson, but Ash Sevo is dead."

No. His heart rebelled against it all; this was no accident. What had happened to Ash, Evie's forgetfulness that night, they weren't intentional, they weren't vicious. But this – oh, this – he could feel it in his gut; something foul had a hand in this. *Someone* foul. His daughter was brash, but she was smart, she'd been brought up around machines all her life. What had happened with Ash, it was the magic that had thrown her, that had caused her mistake. There was no way Evie would be careless when it came down to pure machinery, be it with her own life or another's. Whatever happened, be it fair or ill, he'd find out. He'd find that Shoshanna and make her talk.

"My, that's a wrathful look, Watterson." Friday was looking down at him, arms crossed but face placid. When had she arrived?

"Friday, have you been here this whole time?" A soft grumble sounded from Modesto, but he didn't wake; Watt tightened his hold.

"Unfortunately, but it shouldn't be much longer. They're letting her out now."

"Her? Oh, your Shadow girl."

"Mm." She sat next to him, keeping her voice low. "And how has your morning been so far?"

He looked at her, seeing the strength in her shoulders and hearing the candour in her voice, and decided to repay in kind.

"My daughter's been arrested."

She nodded sagely, sitting back in her chair. "I see."

"They thought your girl was her accomplice."

"Well, they always like to blame her for something."

"Evie didn't do it. That bomb killed the people who put it down; Evie wouldn't have been so sloppy." It was a catharsis, saying it out loud, letting his suspicions out into the air to land where they would. The calmness of Friday's gaze helped.

"Prove it, then."

In the next moment a gate opened across the chamber; a Shadow emerging looking rumpled but unafraid. It was odd, finally seeing this legendary person in the flesh, and as she came closer the stories of her race ran rampant in Watt's mind. The other-worldly green-and-starburst pupils of her eyes were almost enough to banish the image of Evie, though not for long. So this was the Shadow he'd been hearing about, Friday's precious Ridley Ripley. Watt watched, enthralled, as Friday crowded into her space, a finger under the woman's chin as she looked her over. Ridley huffed.

"Do I meet your standards, Captain?"

Friday growled, flicking Ridley on the nose as she stepped back. "Don't you play those games with me, Ridley Ripley."

Snuffling beside him stole his attention; Watt couldn't help a small smile as Modesto blinked awake.

"All right there, sleeping beauty?"

The confusion on the younger man's face would have made him laugh any other time, but his grief wouldn't allow it.

"How long was I asleep?"

"Not quite an hour."

"Oh." Obviously forgetting himself, Modesto stretched, Watt wincing in sympathy as the former was given a stark reminder. "Fucking ow."

"Have I apologised for breaking your hand again? I should probably stop doing that."

Modesto snorted, wriggling his fractured fingers experimentally.

"Stop that."

"I think I'll let you off this time. But my bones and I kindly request there not be a third time – oh."

Watt swivelled, following Modesto's gaze to find Roman staring at them, grave of face but welcome all the same.

"Deputy Commissioner–"

She stepped to him quickly, leaning in close as he stood to meet her.

"Roman?"

"Come with me, just you. Modesto needs to stay here."

Watt looked to his friend, the younger man frowning where he sat.

"What's going on?"

Watt shook his head, Modesto's growl rumbling to silence, not that his current state did much to threaten anyhow.

"We have to be quick, I'm sorry." She spun around without another word, and he didn't linger.

"Stay with Friday, Mods." He didn't hear his friend's answer, or Friday's assurance, if she'd given one at all. All he could focus on was Roman's grey clad back leading him into the bowels of the Highfort, steps measured in their immediacy. They passed through a number of doors that swung of their own accord, and Watt was sure he heard the grinding of locks behind him as they went. A few Greycoats gave them a brief glance as they passed by, but none seemed remotely inclined to stop them.

Eventually they stopped before a door, thick and dark and fearsome in the way only inanimate objects could be.

"Roman?"

"Go on, but don't waste time with the niceties. The commissioner doesn't find out about this." With the barest twitch of her hand the door opened, revealing a dim room containing little more than a bench, a set of bars and the unmistakable shape of his daughter.

"Evie!" When their eyes met something came to life within him, hands going beyond the bars to meet hers before he realised he'd moved at all.

"Dad!"

He looked her over, covered in soot and dirt as she obviously had been since the news broke. Her expression was wild, hair greasy and tangled, but he'd recognise her anywhere.

"Evie, what in Io fucking Sola have you done? Why are they saying you're responsible for all this?"

She gripped his hand tighter, wildness settling down under his scrutiny.

"Because I am."

No, he wouldn't accept that. Evie was not a killer, Evie was not Evelyn. But the rebuttal caught in his throat.

"I made those bombs. I admit it. But no one was meant to die."

He ripped his hands away, the image of Ash's coffin flashing through his mind. *No one is ever meant to die…*

"What the fuck did you think was going to happen? Bombs kill people, Evie, it's what they're made for. It's their design. Hasn't Modesto taught you that by now?"

She looked abashed for a moment, delicate-looking hands turning white round the bars of her cell. When she looked up, though, well, he couldn't keep her gaze. She looked just like him.

"They were only meant to scare the Greycoats, the Citadel. Shoshanna and I made them to distract – to disturb, organised chaos – but I suppose it doesn't matter. Not now. People are dead, the cause is tainted."

"Of course it matters, Evie. You can attest to what you like, but you made weapons. You don't get to be surprised when someone uses them."

"Dad, listen to me. No one was meant to die, no one. Maria was in charge of making sure the targets were empty, and when I found out what Shoshanna was planning I–"

"Shoshanna?" Well, he'd a good instinct in him after all. "What the fuck has she done?"

"She planned it, Dad, Shoshanna lied to us all, to me. When I found out I tried to stop them but by the time I got there the bomb had gone off; the others were already dead."

He watched her closely, the indignation vibrating under her skin so clearly he could make it out in the gloom.

"And the Shadow?"

Evie groaned, head lolling onto those damn bars. "I suppose she's just an easy monster to make."

Footsteps sounded outside but the door remained closed, and he recalled Roman's words; they didn't have long.

"Look, Evie, this has to be quick. If I can do anything–"

"You can." Their eyes met, the panic long gone from her expression. "I told her about Modesto."

"What do you mean, 'told her'? Told her what?" A chill settled, his limbs heavy as he looked at her. *Don't take this one, Evie...*

"About his designs. About his... his family."

"His fucking family?–"

"Be angry at me once this is over. She'll be at the workshop tomorrow night, Dad; you have to be ready for her."

He didn't hang around after that, Evie's stalwart gaze enough to dispel any ideas he had of hashing things out then and there. She should know better; she should fucking know. There were things they didn't talk about, things they didn't share, and for Evie to be so careless with someone else's secrets, someone else's life… but that was just it. She *was* careless nowadays, and as much as it pained him, he couldn't bring himself to ask her why.

Roman gave him a tight smile when they reached the entrance hall, silently leaving him and disappearing into the Highfort.

Modesto was where Watt had left him, frowning at the floor as Friday and the Shadow sat silently to his right. Watt flinched; Modesto wouldn't react well to what Evie had done. He swallowed the words down – it was best the younger man never knew.

"Ready to get home?"

"Watt." Three red heads turned to him, one far more startling. Modesto grimaced as he rose and Watt's fingers itched to reach out and touch him, but guilt stayed his hand. "Is Evie all right?"

Watt shrugged. "She's well enough. We need to go home." He held up a hand at Modesto's look. "Sleep first. We'll talk after." He shifted his focus to Friday, who was looking at him in a way he just couldn't decipher.

"Thank you for staying with him."

"Of course, we Harlons stick together." Something odd passed through the three around him, and Watt couldn't decipher that either.

"What are you doing now, going home?"

Friday slipped her hand into Ridley's, speaking passively. "Our home is a crime scene, and I'm not convinced of its safety right now. I'd rather not end up here again today."

Watt frowned, taking in Ridley's silent tension.

"You think they'll come back and finish what they started?"

When those eyes met his it took everything not to gasp; the depths of those broken pupils unfathomable.

"In a sense."

Modesto groaned quietly where stood, Watt ready with a helping hand, only to be batted away.

"I can manage on my own, Watt."

Watt shrugged off his guilt; he'd always been selfish when it came to Modesto. As he placed a hand on the small of the other man's back despite his protestations, Watt gazed earnestly at the two women.

"You're more than welcome to come home with us. You won't be bothered there and we've plenty of space." Modesto stiffened under his hand but he carried on, entreaties continuing. "You'd be a welcome distraction."

"Thank you, Watterson, we accept." Ridley glared as Friday cut her off, but went when she was bid.

As they slowly made their way out of the Highfort, Modesto leant in close. "What are you doing? This is hardly the time for house guests."

"I meant what I said: I need the distraction."

“From thinking about Evie?”

“From all of it, Mods. From this… this perpetual grief we’re stuck in. Gods, I still need to tell Wes and Leon before I can even think of… of anything else.”

“Let me.” The desperation in Modesto’s voice threw him; it would seem he needed to give help as much as receive it. “Please, let me. You’ve done enough.”

Watt acquiesced, happy to let Modesto feel useful when they all felt helpless. He looked at the two women beside them, guilt creeping in on top of everything else. It was cruel to drag them into it, but then, it seemed as though Ridley Ripley had already been snared in whatever was about to unfold. Still, he couldn’t shake the selfishness of his request, but then he couldn’t bring himself to regret it either. They’d be safe now, Modesto and Wes; they’d be all right. No one would dare try to take them from him again, not when he had a Shadow in the house.

Chapter 25

SEV°

Had the Sevos been in Cerrano all those years ago? Had they been one of the first families to settle by the lake? Ridley certainly couldn't remember them, but a lot could happen in 170 years. There would have been a power vacuum once she and Friday disappeared, and it seemed some wealthy Ajartans filled it with grand promises and a grander mansion.

"It's a bit much now but it was all the fashion at the time. The Sevo family were big on statements." Watt sounded almost apologetic as he led them in, arm tight around Modesto's waist; they both looked ready to keel over. "Come right in, I'll be back in a minute." With that he tugged an unresisting Modesto up the mighty staircase ahead of them, feet making no sound on the plush carpet.

Ridley's eyes roved over a decadent entrance hall, walls and floors a dark, rich wood, accented with deep red carpets. Heavy curtains framed mighty windows, the largest of which looked out onto a vibrant garden. There were on paintings on all the walls, carvings in the ceiling and, strangest of all, potted plants on every available surface.

"Those are Wes'. He's developed quite an affection for plants." Leon's voice carried softly in the stillness as she emerged from a side door. She caught Friday's smile from the corner of her eye.

"I didn't know you lived here."

"Technically I don't, but needs must. What brings you by this morning?"

"Watterson invited us to stay, just till the tower is back to normal." *Till they've scraped melted man off the floorboards and scrubbed away Lara's blood.* So, Leon didn't know, or at least, she didn't seem worried by what was going on out in the city.

"I see."

Their voices faded out as Ridley allowed her tiredness to engulf her; sleep, sleep would be nice. Although the spots of tightened skin on her hands and neck served as an irritating reminder that Lara was still streaked all over her, along with the acrid smell of burning flesh stubbornly refusing to leave her nostrils. By Teala, she needed a bath.

By the time she registered Friday's hand in hers she was up the stairs, Leon leading them deeper into the house. Passing by the corridor windows she managed a real glimpse of the garden, a bold heart in the middle of the mansion, huge glass ceiling letting in streams of sunlight. Down amongst the leaves she spotted a boy, lovingly working away.

"Here we are, our best guest room."

They entered a chamber bedecked in the softest shades of mint and cream she'd ever seen, everything light and gilded along the edges. Golden vines trailed along the walls and were stitched into fabrics. Ridley felt Friday's disgust pouring off her in waves.

"Make yourselves at home, there's a working shower just through that door." Staying with the founders of the Steam Syndicate was bound to have its advantages. Who was Ash Sevo to deny himself and his guests such easily crafted luxuries? "I'll leave you both to it; if you need anything don't hesitate to ask."

If she weren't already done for the day Ridley might have read more into the look Leon gave her; as it was, she hadn't the energy to do more than store it away. Finally left alone with Friday, she wasted no time in ridding herself of her tainted clothes, flesh pulling as the fabric was encrusted from dried blood. The nervous energy of her magic had long since faded till it was like it'd never been there at all, the only vestiges of the attack the lingering smell of burning skin. And here she'd thought Cerrano to be different. Hurrying into the washroom, clothes a dirty trail behind her, she was greeted with a prettily tiled little room smelling of honey and lavender. It was such a soft, sweet scent she didn't realise it'd overtaken her till she was fiddling with the taps, taking a deep breath only to find the gut-churning stench of crispy flesh had faded away. Her tremors stopped, calm lending deftness to her movements that saw her swiftly under a stinging hot spray. Away went the blood and dirt, the evidence of Lara's life dripping off her skin and swirling down the drain.

Scrubbed a healthy pink and lungs full of steam,

Ridley emerged, damp and tired but calmer than before. The towel she wrapped herself in was so soft she couldn't help but let out a sigh, burrowing her nose into the fabric. Reluctantly she moved to the mirror, feet slapping against the tiled floor as the sound echoed round the room. Her limbs were steady, skin clean, and without wasting a moment she wiped a hand over the glass.

Ridley kept her eyes on her fingers, finding the end of her largest scar and following the platinum vein up the inside of her wrist to her inner elbow where it met others, getting wider and whiter as it led up till, finally, she reached the mess atop her heart. All the little lightning bolts, thin rivers of glaring brightness stretching across collarbones and down ribs in an electric dance. It was worse in the mirror, the scar whiter against her heated skin. Perhaps she'd have another one before this mess was through. Or perhaps there'd be no more scars.

Friday was lying in bed when she emerged, staring at the door with docile eyes. Her strewn-about clothing had disappeared; knowing the older woman, they'd probably been burned. Ridley paused at the foot of the bed.

"Tired?"

"Aren't you?"

She shrugged. "I think I may have passed that."

"Come to bed anyway. Our sleeping patterns won't right themselves now."

She wanted to, oh, how she wanted to, but unsaid words locked her muscles.

Friday frowned sadly. "It'll be OK, you know. It always is."

She wouldn't argue the lie, she didn't need to; to Friday words were simply noise.

"All right." As her body sunk into the bed warmth crept in, Friday's hand finding hers under the covers. Ridley shuffled closer, pressing her nose to the other woman's shoulder and murmuring into her skin. "I didn't mean what I said."

Friday's arm wound around her waist, legs tangling together as she pressed a gentle kiss against Ridley's hair.

"I know, girl, neither did I."

Coming back to consciousness was a wearisome affair, her eyelids needing a stern mental talking-to before they cracked open. Blinking sluggishly, Ridley sat up, Friday still sleeping on beside her, peaceful and unburdened. The Shadow smiled, taking in the sight with a heart that felt light despite her troubles. Tucking the image away, she quietly climbed out of bed, finding only Friday's clothes to pull on. They were too long by far, and a little broad across the shoulders and hips, but needs must. She'd find them some more somewhere.

The corridors were quiet as she went, tread light on the carpets, each step sending dust dancing in the streams of light from the windows. Watterson was somewhere in the house, he'd know if her clothes had survived Friday's fury, but where? By the gods, the place was huge.

"Ridley Ripley?"

She whipped around, heart pounding at the unfamiliar voice, but it was just a boy.

"Wes Sevo?" He was transfixed as he approached, big, dark eyes never leaving hers. "I'm looking for Watterson, would you please tell me where he is?"

"You're not scary at all."

She quirked a brow, staring down at him with a poorly concealed smile.

"You don't think so?" He shook his head and came closer, the frown on his face deepening as he did so. "Are you all right?"

"You're meant to be really powerful, aren't you? Powerful enough to do almost anything."

"I'm sorry?"

"Can you bring someone back to life?"

Her mouth went dry, staring down at this sad boy with growing horror. Children always asked for the worst things.

"No. Only necromancers can do that."

"Aren't you a necromancer?"

"Shadows are changers."

"So change it: change death to life."

"It doesn't work that way."

"Why not?" He stamped his foot, sounding so young but looking well beyond his years.

She spoke softly, centuries of life giving her patience enough. "Necromancers don't change, they play, and the game must be fair. The debt has to be paid."

He huffed forcibly, staring at the floor till, suddenly, he rushed forward. "You can't change death, but you can prevent it, can't you? Stop it? You could live forever if you wanted."

She felt sick. "Those are just rumours–"

"Alchemists change magic, all alchemists are changers. Can you make a non-magical person magical?"

"In theory."

"How much?" By the Mother, this was why she never wanted children.

"How much what?"

"How much for you to make Mods and Watt and Evie like Andromeda?"

"Like Andro… you mean impenetrable?"

He nodded vigorously, gabbing her hand in his skinny, clammy one.

"Yes, make them impenetrable so that no one can hurt them ever again. So that no one can take them away from me."

Chapter 26

ROMAN CANDLE

"I'm beginning to think you're doing it deliberately." Hadren wasn't glaring exactly, but there was a distinct glowering aspect to the look she currently sported, eyes boring into Lara from across the room. Her voice absolutely did not tremble, although it was rather close.

"Do what?"

"Disobey."

Lara winced – if this was Hadren's reaction, what on Eera was Jackie going to do?

"Are you trying to get thrown out? Or is this some weird game to impress Andromeda?"

"What? No, I don't want to leave."

"Well, that's not how it's coming across."

She turned away, focusing on the deftness of her fingers as she laced up her boots. How could Hadren think she didn't want to be there? That she wanted to go back to Bound? She'd rather be sent to Princetown, locked away with the worst Gallow had to offer, than go back to that place.

The bed dipped beside her but she refused to look up, feeling Hadren close by her elbow.

"Explain it to me, then."

"I can't."

"We're meant to be partners. When Commander King demands to know where you are and I can't answer, how do you think that makes me look? Partners are meant to look after each other, but you keep making that really fucking hard."

She hadn't considered that, assuming Hadren was safe doing her duty, far from Lara's orbit of chaos. But it seemed there was more collateral damage to be discovered.

"I didn't mean to get you in trouble."

"I doubt you meant to get your back split open either, yet here we are." The skin was still aggravatingly itchy; if she looked it'd probably still be viciously red in all the wrong places. Fucking Shoshanna. "Anyway, let's go. Can't be late for the assembly." Hadren held out a hand, which Lara gratefully accepted.

"No, can't be late."

All the Greycoats had gathered in the main courtyard, a pulsating throng of iron awaiting their leader's words. Up ahead Lara spied Roman and the commissioner talking at the edge of the platform, each animated in whatever they were saying. A strong hand hooked into her elbow suddenly, painful tug taking her away from Hadren. She glanced up, meeting eyes woefully similar to her own.

"Commander King."

"Key." Jackie's face was all hard edges, mouth set so grim that the colour had pressed from her lips. "After this, you and I need to have a very serious discussion. Perhaps our last. I cannot fathom what possessed you, of all people, to disobey a direct order, but I assure you I won't waste my time thinking on it."

"I apologise again, ma'am, but–"

"The information you gathered is not in question here, Key, simply your methods in collecting it. As defenders of law and order the latter has to take precedent. Now go. I shall call on you later."

A hollow feeling settled in her chest as she watched Jackie merge into the murmuring crowd. So that's all they were: defenders of law, keepers of order. And here Lara had wanted to defend the people. What would become of her now?

"All at attention for High Commissioner Stone."

To think, the last time she'd seen Jackie King on that stage, she'd thought her a beacon of familiarity, only to discover how painfully right that assumption had been. Lara barely heard the commissioner speak, watching those lips move without a care; what a difference not even two months could make. Her gaze flittered around till, finally, it landed on Roman, whose eyes met her own. It was as though a thousand words flew through the air between them, the deputy commissioner's gaze turning soft and sad.

Stone's words slithered into her consciousness, familiar sounds catching her attention.

"Through diligent, tireless efforts following these incidents, we now have reason to believe the liberationist movement are responsible for the attacks. Our earlier predictions about a magic-user being to blame were down to a false trail of evidence planted by the real culprits, culminating in the deaths of three of their own. As such, all known liberationists must be brought in for questioning, and are to be treated as highly dangerous. In particular, one by the name of–"

Her ears were ringing; a high-pitched wail reverberated round her skull as her mind tried to right itself. There was dust, dirt and shattered bricks filling the air all around. Lara's heart hammered against her chest; she could feel it punching bone but the familiar rhythm was lost beneath that echoing screech. Heat licked at her face, close enough for the sweating to begin, for her uniform to feel stifling. Debris bit into her hands, but it was only a dull ache, much like the throb of long-healed bone. The itching across her back stopped. As she stumbled upright the world returned, each little piece slotting together haphazardly till it made wretched sense.

Orders and shouting and fire, blood on grey and walls tumbled down to rubble beneath her feet. The courtyard was in ruins, and all around fellow officers fought for it. She spied Dory hurrying through a gap with his dogs, barking loud and viciously. Hadren was dancing with the fire, bringing it to her and tamping it down.

It was Roman, blood and dirt caked in that golden face, who summoned Lara like a martyr to a pyre. Roman, down on one knee and grimacing in pain, who, single-handedly, had summoned great roots from the ground to hold up the Highfort's crumbling walls. The closer Lara got the more blood she could see, catching in eyelashes and soaking through that hard-earned uniform.

The mighty tendrils of earth held fast, but Roman was weakening, body buckling under the weight of them all. A section of wall, held only by a small branch, began to fall; Roman holding steadfast in her spot. Lara saw Modesto again on the floor, saw Ridley alone against the horde, and without hesitation she moved. All the strength she possessed, every last shred of hope and want and desire she poured into her muscles. The wall scraped at her bloody palms, body burning under the strain. Her feet skidded in the debris, rocks and destruction only adding to her resistance. Her teeth cracked as she grimaced, tendons and bones just as stubborn as the mind that moved them. With a grunt she stopped the descent, but her body was frozen, spent of its last reserves. The irony, for her to be crushed supporting the organisation that was so ready to throw her off.

Something warm and rough wound about her wrist; a small, slithering vine had come to her aid. *Roman.* She glanced over her shoulder, golden eyes peering out from a curtain of steadily dripping red. The scrap of wood against her scarred knuckles was all she needed, her leader's faith pulsating into her skin and lending a burst of strength. With an almighty cry Lara surged forward, pushing the wall up and into place, stone settling as though it'd no intention of doing anything else.

She burned as she knelt, energy expended and body weary beyond belief, but she couldn't stop. Ignoring the shooting pain in her limbs she crawled across the rubble, reaching Roman just in time to catch her as she collapsed. Blood and heat seeped into her clothes, breath stuttering as she sought to support them both.

"Roman?"

"Lara…"

She pulled the older woman to her, shivering at the sensations running through her skin. Noise and heat and images, all the Highfort in its decimated glory filtering through her head. How did Roman live with it?

"She's dead, Lara."

"Who?"

The picture flashed before her, reality falling away beneath it. Commissioner Stone, unmoving, crushed under a chunk of collapsed wall. Suddenly it was gone, Roman sagging in her hold as Lara's senses righted themselves. She looked across the courtyard, to where Jackie and some others were clawing at the rubble, desperate to find their leader. She'd not the heart to tell them they were too late.

Chapter 27

FORMATION

She was still there, Evie, waiting in that shattered monument of stone even as it trembled. He'd been praying to whichever god deigned to listen to send him a reprieve, a distraction from his grief. What a sick sense of humour the divine had. Was she still unhurt? Or had the liberationists and their fanaticism taken even the chance to see her again? His knuckles whitened, window frame creaking under his hold. Did Shoshanna really think this could all go unanswered? Was that cunt so self-assured that she thought Evie would be left to take the fall? That she could come for Modesto? No. It wouldn't stand. Rage thrummed through him, skin vibrating with the intensity of it all. Shoshanna would soon learn just who it was that kept the syndicate growing, that Evie's fire wasn't all of her mother's making; after all, it was his name she had chosen. The Teaches would not be ignored.

A soft knock on his office door quelled his macabre

thoughts; however, Ridley's appearance set his mind to plotting.

"Ridley, what can I do for you?"

She perched on the seat he gestured to; he sat opposite with forced ease. His eyes flickered over the scar on her neck, the tips of her fingers and even her shoes. Important as his plans were, being alone with a Shadow was still a fearsome novelty.

"I was just wondering how you were. It's rather a pathetic question, but some people appreciate it all the same." She didn't sound how he'd imagined; it was the most he'd ever heard her say, yet all he caught were whispered notes of tiredness, each syllable warbling with a bone-deep ache heavier than his own.

"I suppose I'm as could be expected. Once Leon returns with news of Evie and the Highfort it'll all be all right again."

"Of course."

People often spoke about a Shadow's eyes, the deep, rich green that seemed so other-worldly. But as Watt locked gazes with Ridley he realised, sitting so close, that it was the pupils that you fell into; the asymmetric starbursts of black that you couldn't pull away from. They made this woman, who thanked him for his hospitality and enquired about his health, seem… inhuman.

"Wes spoke to me yesterday."

"What about?"

"He's concerned about you and Modesto. He thinks it only a matter of time before you leave him too."

"Evie and Ash didn't leave, they were taken."

"He doesn't see the difference–"

"Well, I do." He leant back, aghast at his own outburst. Calming the hostility broiling in his gut was getting harder, each new tragedy and insult stoking it. She'd been nothing but cordial, though, still looking unharried by his heated words.

"Evie's not dead, Watterson, she's still very much alive."

"And if they send her to Princetown? How well do you think someone without magic will do in there?"

She shrugged. "I'm a Shadow, not a fortune teller."

He couldn't fathom her, this inscrutable woman who willed him to openness. She spoke as though…

"You're rather young to be so cynical."

"I'm older than I look."

"How old exactly?"

"Seven hundred and eighteen."

"Fine, don't tell me."

"And how old are you, Teach?"

"I'll be forty-two at the end of spring."

She nodded shallowly, turning suddenly to the window. "I can't believe it's so early in the year; not even Midspring yet."

He followed her gaze to the window, staring out at the morning and seeing, full and bright in the sky, the sun unhindered by cloud. Usually Wes counted down the days till their birthdays, always insisting on doing something special, but not this year.

"It's not been much of a year for celebrations. Ash died at the end of Lythra and after that, well… He was always the one for parties; he wanted to do a big New Year's celebration. Fireworks, sparklers; anything that made people warm in the snow." The smile that came to his lips was sad, the corners of his mouth barely mustering the energy to lift.

"That's sweet."

"Maybe. That's how I'll remember it regardless."

If he'd let them, those happy thoughts would consume him, ensconce him in warm memories and make a mockery of the righteous indignation he'd managed to build. So, with a heavy heart, he put them away; Ash's memory was not to be tarnished by what he had to do.

"Ridley, I've a favour to ask."

The quirk of her smile disappeared, indifference settling in. "Yes, I thought you might."

"You did?"

"It's nothing against you personally, but I learned long ago that no one invites a Shadow into their house without a reason."

He didn't feel any better for her words; fulfilling someone's low expectations was hardly a point of pride.

"What is it you want?"

He took a deep breath, and set his story to rights. "I'm going to catch Shoshanna, and I need your help to do it."

"I see."

"She's running out of materials – she'll come to the HQ tonight and try to gather more."

"And what makes you so sure? She could wait it out, you could be wrong about her."

"I'm not. Evie told me."

"And you believe her?"

"Yes." It was the easiest thing in the world to say now, all those worries and fears eaten up by faith. Evie was good; he needed no more proof than her word. "She's getting bolder, and the Greycoats won't rest till they've locked up every liberationist in the city. She *will* come tonight to get what she needs."

Ridley cocked her head. "And you require what of me?"

"Protection."

"Protection? If you want a guard then you'd be better off with Lara–"

"Shoshanna is frightened of you. Why do you think she had her people attack you?"

"I'm well aware of how terrifying you all find me. But surely my presence will only make things more dangerous."

"I'm counting on it–"

"You want me to kill them."

The silence that descended was a sharp, deadly thing; yet what could he say that would prove her wrong? She scowled at him, but there was no real bite to it.

"I've had quite enough of being weaponised for one lifetime, Watterson Teach."

"I'm not asking you to–"

"Yes, you are."

She stood slowly, as though all her movements were weighted by some invisible force. "There's an irony that it falls to me to say this, but Modesto and Wes love you, and they deserve more than to be left to tell your daughter she can't be there when they bury you."

Watt shifted, chair suddenly uncomfortable. "I know."

"Then I'm with you, if only to keep you alive. I keep my promises."

She left him there, slouched in his seat and breathing heavily. He swallowed back the sob that threatened; his grief would have to wait a little longer.

Wes had a tight hold on Modesto, fingers pale under the pressure. He hadn't spoken, hadn't cried; he'd just taken hold of Modesto's arm and refused to let go ever since. Watt couldn't take his eyes off the boy; unending litany of Ash Sevo is dead *on a loop in his mind. Smoke inhalation, they had said; he'd fallen asleep up in the office – not felt a thing; just slept, breaths eventually tapering off. No pain, they'd said – but it felt wrong. Ash was loud and bright and so very alive in everything he did. For his death to be so quiet, so… nothing; it was all wrong.*

Evie was strong beside him; sat up straight and conversing in hurried, hushed whispers with Leon. Poor Leon; she'd not signed up for this. And Evie, what could he say to her, how could he explain? He couldn't. He just couldn't, they'd lost too much already; he couldn't lose any more. By the Mother, what would Modesto say, or Wes? He focused on them again, on the silent despair permeating the room, dripping from them both and eating up the air. He needed to tell someone; he needed to tell Modesto.

"Mods, can I talk to you for a moment? In the other room?"

Modesto looked pained, peering down at Wes and swallowing heavily. The boy hadn't seemed to notice, still clinging and staring into the distance.

"Right now?"

Watt nodded, the pain shooting down his spine. "It's important."

"OK, um...–"

"Wes, do you want to come sit by me?" Evie's voice cut through the air, the boy blinking into life. "Mods and Dad need to deal with some things, you don't want to get in their way."

Watt watched Wes' fingers tighten enough to bruise, lower lip trembling. He moved forward.

"We'll just be through that door; you'll still be able to see us. All right?"

Eventually they managed to pry Modesto free, Wes sitting forlornly between Evie and Leon, looking smaller than he ever had. Watt pulled the door half shut, giving Wes a tight smile as he did so. Wearily he turned to his friend, who looked as worn down as he felt. He took a deep breath – best to get it done quickly.

"A burner was left on."

"A burner? But they all get switched off automatically."

"It was the new magical one we've been testing."

"It still should have been turned off, that's why –" That tempestuous mouth slammed shut, lips paling to match his skin. "Oh."

Suddenly there were arms around Watt, that familiar warmth diffusing into his chilled bones.

"I'm sorry, Watt."

His heart cracked a little more. He slowly brought his own arms up, encircling that body he knew so well, hands clenching the fabric of Modesto's nightshirt. He'd forgotten, they'd been asleep two hours ago.

"Who else knows?"

Reluctantly he pulled back, meeting those melancholy green eyes as a shudder ran through him.

"Leon's the one who told me, she went in and looked for herself. She told the Greycoats that Ash had left it on, but..."

"She knew."

Watt nodded. "She knew."

He pressed a quick kiss on the corner of Modesto's mouth, no more than a simple brush of his bitten lips against that rough skin. Watt didn't say it, there was no need, but he knew Modesto knew. It passed between them like everything meaningful always had: quietly and without violence. Leon wouldn't tell, she'd no reason to; Evie's mistake would be just another untold thing for them to share.

Chapter 28

FRIDAY'S GIRL

There'd be shouting soon enough when Modesto learned of their plans, when Friday found out. But not yet. Ridley would give herself enough peace and quiet to level out, and then face Friday. For once she knew what to say, knew how to word everything and, despite what had gone before, she wasn't worried. What would be would be; all she needed to focus on was keeping Watterson alive. She knew well enough his mindset, his half-assed rationalisations, but if Ridley had to live, then so did Teach. She'd promised the boy after all.

Someone was behind her, Leon emerging from a side door with quiet steps. It felt strange to be alone with her after all this time with barely two words passing between them, and even then, Friday tended to answer. Yet here they were, just the two of them, staring at each other in a quiet hall. It was Leon who eventually broke the silence.

"Wes told me what he asked of you."

Ridley remained silent, leaning back against the wall and breathing in the scent of peonies that flowered around the windows.

"He also told me your counter-offer. That was very kind of you, although I doubt Watt and Modesto will appreciate a keeper."

Ridley nodded but didn't move otherwise; from the woman's fidgeting she could tell Leon had something to say, something important. Ridley didn't want to put her off.

"You don't remember me, do you?" Well, that wasn't what she expected. "At first I thought you were embarrassed, but then I realised you didn't recognise me. Not even my name."

"I'm sorry, I wasn't aware we'd met."

"No, neither did Friday at first. I'd thought she'd have told you by now, though."

Ridley ran an assessing eye over Leon, taking in the sharp eyes and full mouth.... Something familiar stirred.

"We've just been a bit preoccupied..."

"Yes, yes, of course you have." Leon huffed, squaring her shoulders. "We met over twenty years ago, down in Orysan. My mother is Sylph Tsaika, and my father is–"

"Carvelt Leon." Shit, no wonder Leon looked at Ridley like something feral through a glass; she'd seen her at her worst. "You were there."

"I was there."

All her calm was carried away on those whispered words, Leon's face morphing before her into a rounder, younger child staring up at her in wonder. She'd been so low in Orysan, lower even than Vincent. The weight of those forgotten feelings crawled like spiders up her limbs, the shadow of that unconquerable ache reminding her just how low she could get. The scar still throbbed sometimes, veins recalling the agony of white-hot lightning dancing through them. How strange, she always thought it, that her skin should so clearly bear the evidence of what had gone on beneath.

"I'm sorry if I upset you, I'm not trying to dredge up bad memories." She looked sincere enough, but Ridley still felt too big for her skin. Suddenly Leon's proximity stung.

"Then what did you want?"

"I've grown to consider Friday a friend."

Ridley bristled; Leon had no idea what she was barging into.

"And though it's become more and more clear to me that you and I shall never share that title, I can't deny you're the thing she loves most in the world."

"I'm aware of Friday's feelings–"

"Then I'm asking you, since you know how she feels, not to put her through that pain again. You may not remember me, but I remember you. I remember how you were back then, and no matter what Watt has asked you to do tonight, it doesn't have to end the way it did then."

Ridley flinched, the searing feel of electricity pulsing through her heart nothing to the image of Friday's face. She couldn't forget the taste of the poison she'd drunk, the sting as Friday pulled the rod from her chest, the hacking as she coughed up all that blood and the heat, oh, the heat as the energy went through her… but it was Friday, quiet and clinging, that was clearest of all. In the days that followed she'd felt scraped raw, soul confused and clawing at her thin, battered skin. Even weeks later, when she'd been well enough to leave that cursed country, Friday had barely spoken to her. It'd taken them months to get back on track, to reclaim who they were to each other. Each time, each attempt had a longer fallout; one more and maybe Friday would stop forgiving her.

Ridley stood tall, hands clenched as she moved away. Neither spoke, silence her only companion as she walked away.

The shouting started before she found Friday, stamping feet and slamming doors signalling Modesto's take on the night's planned events; not that Watt didn't deserve it. Ideas and justifications sat heavy on her when she saw Friday, sat in the garden looking like some wintry rose that'd lost its way. She sat up as Ridley approached, smiling brightly.

Ridley didn't hesitate. "I don't want to die here." Friday blinked, opening her mouth to reply, but Ridley cut her off. "I just wanted you to know that."

"That's very thoughtful of you."

"And I'll do everything in my power to make sure I don't, which is considerable, so you can be assured I'll still be here tomorrow. And the day after. And all the days that follow if that's what you want. All right?"

A grin split Friday's face, eyes twinkling like gleaming steel. "You're about to do something stupid, aren't you?"

"Yes, but I wanted you to know that I'll still be here for you to shout at afterwards."

Friday stood, moving so there was nothing between them but heat and shared breaths.

"Girl, you're the only creature in the world that means more proclaiming you'll live for me rather than die for me."

"You didn't seem to like it when I died."

"That is not funny."

Ridley smiled, burrowing her face against Friday's neck and breathing deep of the scent of the cold.

"You should have told me about Leon."

"Probably, but I think I love you too much."

"You think? It's been almost seven hundred years; shouldn't you know by now?"

Ridley inclined her head up, Friday answering her silent question with a light kiss, pulling away despite the younger woman's groan of protest.

"You can have another when you tell me this plan of yours."

"Fine. But if you don't like it I still want my payment."

Chapter 29

HAVOC

The unsettling similarities between Friday and Modesto were only more apparent when they stood next to each other: their colouring, their stature, the unending whiplash of their emotions. In the little time Lara had spent with them, however, she'd noticed one fundamental difference: resolve. Whereas Friday, when faced with Ridley's apathy, would argue till she succeeded, Modesto's fire was quicker to extinguish under Watt's stubbornness. There was a streak of vulnerability to him that appeared worryingly easy to exploit if tonight was anything to go by. Even with that in mind, watching the two of them converse left her feeling as though she were on shaky ground. Lara wasn't ashamed to admit that Friday still terrified her.

"Are you listening to me, Lara?"

She shuddered as Andromeda's breath ghosted over her ear.

"Only you look a little lost."

"I'm just wondering how I ended up here." It was a good question, yet one which she was incapable of answering even with all the facts in her possession. Andromeda had found her after the explosion, still caked in Roman's blood and feeling more alive than ever. It was astounding how swiftly the power had returned to her body, limbs vibrating with adrenaline and opportunity. Whatever strength Roman had lent her hadn't diminished; she'd something primal in her veins now.

"You got here by volunteering, remember? You wanted to tear Shoshanna's arms off, or something equally graphic."

Lara huffed. "I know how I got here, Andy; I meant how did I get *here*?" She nodded her head towards the still-talking pair, and Andromeda smirked.

"Do they make you uncomfortable?"

"Actually, I think it might be the other way around."

She couldn't be sure of course, but however nervous Lara felt, there seemed to be a similar sense of unease radiating from Modesto and Friday. It could have been the situation, but she really felt as though her presence unnerved them just as much as theirs did her. Well, if the uniform was the issue, it wouldn't be a problem much longer. Saving Roman hadn't softened Jackie's attitude towards her, and Lara had left the Highfort that evening with a settled resolve. She'd show them just who they were giving up on.

"We're meant to be working together, but they haven't even looked at us."

Andromeda hummed. "I suppose they're worried."

"We're all worried."

"Yes, but I'd be rather testy if *you'd* gone on with Ripley and Watterson."

Lara couldn't help her smirk, warmth blooming in her chest as she leant in to Andromeda.

"You like me."

The older girl rolled her eyes at the sing-song sound of Lara's voice, quickening her steps. "You're such a child."

"And yet you adore me – hey, I'm only two years younger than you..."

Her voice petered out as the syndicate HQ came into view, the outside appearing far less innocuous now she knew who was waiting inside.

"And here I'd hoped Cerrano would be a fresh start..."

Lara turned to glance at Friday, who was smiling sadly up at the sky. High above, the half-crescent moon of the Mother waxed bright blue; the small, white moon of the Child safely beside it. She used to stare up at them in Bound and count her life away: *Just two more moons till the year's over... one more year down till my life begins.* Now here she was, watching them again, waiting.

When she looked back, Friday's eyes were fixed firmly upon her. "You seem apt at attracting trouble, Lara Key."

"Apparently."

"Good, then go get in trouble." Friday nodded at Modesto, standing to her full height. "If there's a bomb in there I'll take care of it. You three draw whatever attention you can to yourselves, give Watt and Ridley a clear path to Shoshanna. You all try at least somewhat not to get killed, all right? I'm sure there are people who'd miss you all." Her last words she levelled at Modesto, who merely grunted as they watched her go.

Quietly as they could, the three of them headed into the warehouse, ears pricked for the sounds of trouble. As they went, Lara had a thought, whispering to Andromeda.

"What's Friday's gift?"

"Pardon?"

"Her magic, what is it?"

"Umm..."

"She's a metal-twister." Modesto and those green eyes of his gleamed in the shadows, voice tight. "She doesn't need our help, and neither do the others. But we're helping anyway." There was that vulnerability again, the sorrowful note that anchored his voice. Lara couldn't fathom how to deal with it, but luckily Andromeda's presence meant she didn't have to.

"I'd rather they didn't need us. Mother knows what might happen if our lives depended on Lara."

"Hey...–"

Her rebuttal was cut short by the appearance of a figure up ahead, moving conspicuously along the walls. Modesto's growl grumbled low.

"We need to get closer, see how many there are."

Lara clutched the man's sleeve, freeing herself of all that earlier humour. "Stay behind us once it starts, you're most at risk here."

"Me? What about you? They got you once already–"

"Yes, but I'm still kicking. They won't get another shot."

If there was one thing Lara's handlers had always praised her for, it was her ability to remember her mistakes – in battle at least. They'd hit Lara once; now it was her turn, and with Roman's power still snapping through her synapses they'd rue the day they left her alive.

"I'm not saying don't fight, just stick close to Andromeda; leave violence to the dogs." Without waiting she slunk forward, hearing them close behind.

The person up ahead went back the way they'd come, footsteps echoing down the corridor. Through an open doorway Lara saw them, nine people stood staring at all the entrances, postures rigid with anticipation. She could practically smell the adrenaline, each as eager for a fight as the next. Well, if it was a brawl they wanted, Lara would give them their chance for blood. She spoke quietly, keeping her gaze sharp.

"There's nine in there, Andy. I'll go at them first, you and Modesto watch my back. Deal with any that manage to get by me."

"Lara?" A soft hand slipped into hers, warmth close against her back. "No killing, all right? I know you're angry for Roman and the commissioner, but you're an officer of the law–"

"Funny, yesterday I would have agreed with you."

With Andromeda's questioning look still in her head, Lara let her instincts take over, that lingering touch of gold gifting her movements with self-assured strength. She cast off her worries, grey jacket sliding from her shoulders so easily she wondered if she'd ever cared for it at all. So she wasn't a Greycoat – it didn't have to be the end. Lara would be her own master, and her first act would be to show these terrorists all the mercy life had deigned to show her.

Their astonishment at her approach was drowned out by a constant buzzing in her head, whatever they had to say muffled and unimportant. Her steps didn't falter for a single second, fist connecting with the closest woman's jaw; delight coursing through her at the crunch of bone as flesh met fist. It was a blur after that, all her pent-up aggression and self-loathing let loose upon these people, this gang who'd thought so little about who might stand in their way. Bones shattered, skin tore, blood splattered warm and wet against her; yet she didn't tire. In her mind's eye she saw Roman peering at her amidst the chaos, heard Hadren's laugh above the yells and felt Andromeda's lips each time a hit touched her.

By the time reality slipped back in and she peered about, there wasn't a trace of pain in her body. Her chest heaved under her blood-soaked vest, fists still raised and ready, but there was no one left to fight. All about her they lay, groaning or silent but otherwise unmoving. Andromeda and Modesto were quiet as they watched her, neither attempting to say a word. Slowly, Lara lowered her hands and laughed.

Chapter 30
VILLAINS

The shouting petered out slowly, crashing and grunts taking its place till eventually even they stopped. In the ensuing silence Ridley watched Watterson pale, muscles fighting mind as they walked quietly through the factory. She knew Modesto would be fine, Friday wouldn't allow anything to happen to him, but the words died on her tongue. Placations were a waste of breath; she could tell Watt wasn't in the frame of mind to appreciate them. He wanted to rage, needed it, he craved the release that might be coming. Ridley knew all too well the catharsis that lay ahead for him; he was too young to regret the things she did.

Tense silence was all that lay between them, violence behind and most likely ahead. Her nerves sang with the waiting, each new sound a possibility to unleash what she locked away so covetously. Watt asked for her help, wanted her protection, but did he really know who he was asking? She watched the stilted way he moved, shoulders and back taut in front of her. Perhaps he'd be less willing to be alone with a Shadow before the night was through.

As the way to Watt's office came into view steps sounded to their left; more than enough pairs of feet to get in their way. Ridley gave Watt a light shove, turning to face the approaching horde.

"Go, I'll deal with this."

"Are you sure?"

"Watterson, Shoshanna came here for a reason. They've been here too long for it just to be a smash-and-grab; she wants to have it out with you."

"Will you be all right, though?" Oh, there was earnestness in his voice. Who'd have thought?

"I can handle a group of have-a-go terrorists. Now go get Shoshanna. And for the Mother's sake, don't die."

His diminishing steps disappeared as the group encroached, angry voices signalling their arrival. She couldn't see exactly how many there were, perhaps twelve or so at a glance. Men and women all looking at her with the same disgusted gaze she'd grown so accustomed to over the years. It was hate-filled, fuelled by the underlying fear they were always so ashamed of; their conviction that the person next to them felt exactly the same the only thing keeping any of them from giving in and running away. The hive mind was so self-assured it made itself forget just why they'd feared her in the first place. Ridley was loath to remind them, but they'd gone too far for another solution.

Squaring her shoulders, she put herself between them and the way Watt had gone, tone firm.

“This is private property, you all need to leave. Now.”

“What? Key not a fearsome enough guard dog, they had to get a monster to take her place?” A woman came forward, no doubt buoyed by the horde at her back, smile biting. “We’ll leave when we’re good and ready, *Shadow*. We’ve unfinished business with these traitors.”

Traitors, is that what Shoshanna thought – but who did she think Watt had betrayed?

“The Steam Syndicate are a neutral faction.”

“And yet here you are. You and Lara bloody Key, probably that Knight too I bet; the Citadel’s little spy.” The group sniggered as they moved in, but she’d not have them at her back. “Tell us, if they’re so neutral, why are you magics all here?”

So that’s what Shoshanna had spun to them: that Watt and Modesto were in league with the Citadel; with the Highfort. What had that meant for Evie? Ridley pushed down her anger; she’d questions of her own, ones that couldn’t wait.

“Is that why you’re all here?”

“What?”

“Is that what Shoshanna told you: that you’re dealing with a band of treacherous inventors?”

A man spoke, one she’d only the faintest sense of seeing before. “We know Teach and Cinnabar are liars–”

“Liars about what? And what about Evie? Is she a liar too?”

Murmurs went through them all, the woman snarling at them to hush.

“Evie lost her nerve.”

“Nerve had nothing to do with it.”

"She was the one who let us in here, who built those bombs. What came after was her fault, she's the reason Maria and Wilke died–"

"She went in there to stop them, to save them. Don't pretend you don't know that's the truth of it."

When none of them faltered she realised, painfully, just how deep in Shoshanna's web they were. The unflinching conviction never changed, no matter the country, no matter the century; violence always followed.

Gradually her rage bubbled, a haze the likes of which she'd not seen for centuries descending. She'd been so afraid when Lara had gone down, let her burst of fear boil that man till he was a blistering heap, but this was different. She felt no fear now, no apprehension for what could befall these people. Suddenly she was back on the battlefield, Harleon to the east and red-stained snow underfoot.

"I take it these accusations all come from your fearless leader?"

"Yes." It was the man again. She still didn't recognise him; no doubt he'd been staring at her during the rally, eyes wide before the Greycoats came. "She warned us about you too."

"Did she?"

"Told us not to be fooled by the stories; your people might have been fearsome once, but not any more. You're all withered away, nothing to fear from a half-person whose power lies only in their name."

"Half-person?" Her fists clenched, nails biting pink into pale skin.

"That's why your people all went mad back in the

wars, sold your souls to the goddess Fortella for magic, and you still fucking lost. No victory, no power, no fear."

Had the legends mutated so much, or was this just Shoshanna's doing? Not that it mattered now. It started slow, the feel of magic coursing through her body, jumping over synapses and skipping through her nerves. So much her people had given, *she* had given, and for what? No matter what Friday said, it was too late to change the song now; the world could never be grateful. But by every god in Crescen Iona, she'd make them afraid, make them respectful. If the villain makes the story, then she'd be such a villain no little upstart cunt would dare to laugh at the Shadows again. She growled as she spoke, teeth on display.

"Are your memories so fucking short that you've already forgotten what happened to your mouthy friend the last time you came at me?"

The woman stepped back, but she didn't back down. "That was a one-off, no one's powerful enough to do that again so quickly–"

"Is that what your precious Shoshanna told you?"

Silence descended; none of them moved. Ridley ran an appraising eye over them all, noting with spiteful relief that they looked just as steadfast as before. She let the twisted grin take over, body so replete with power it thrummed.

It was over in a split second, the magic moving about the room like a vicious wave, leaving her and the room coated in a copious layer of blood. It stained her clothes, sat thick and hot on her skin and dripped down from the ceiling to create ripples in the pools across the floor.

The smell, metallic and rich, hit her nostrils all at once. She gagged, tasting a heavy, cloying layer on her tongue, seeping into her through every pore.

The tacky feeling on her skin sucked all her rage away, leaving her hollow and raw, as if all that blood was her own. Glancing down, she caught her reflection in the glossy crimson surface, pristine amongst all the carnage she'd wrought. As she stared, a clawing, yearning desire came over her. The face looking up morphed into one not her own, till she found her sister's eyes. How she longed to hear that voice again. The need ached deep enough that her knees trembled with it, tired soul begging her to just kneel down and let the blood enfold her in its warm embrace.

A drop fell, the image rippling out of existence. Ridley forced herself to turn away. After all, she'd made a promise; she couldn't die today.

Chapter 31

WATTERSON

He was afraid now, walking alone towards his office. Frightened of what he might have to do. The solace in vengeance came from the act itself, enacting whatever violence was necessary with his own two hands – but he wasn't a violent man. Nor were Ash and Modesto, not really. Temperamental perhaps, but no more than a harsh word a swift apology could fix. And yet, as he came closer and closer to his office door, Watt couldn't help but be horrified at his actions of late. He'd buried his grief so deep he hadn't recognised anyone else's. He'd hurt Modesto, ignored Wes, overwhelmed Leon and watched Evie run amok when he knew, felt deep in his bones, that something was wrong. Even now, in the hour of action with all his wrath and rage, he'd expected Ridley to do the dirty work.

He felt sick. What was wrong with him – he looked at the Shadow and saw only what she could do for him. Help him, protect him, kill for him. Gods, he hoped he could spare her that at least. If the legends about her people were true then surely she could incapacitate people without killing them? Yes. Yes, he'd give Ridley that; save her from having to take a life. No one but Shoshanna had to die today. And she would, he'd do that for Evie. If there was one thing he knew about his daughter, it was that forgiveness was not in her nature, and so tonight, he would not forgive.

He paused before the door, trembling hand reaching for the knob. No sound came from inside; yet he knew she was there. He took a deep breath, letting the oxygen buoy him up as much as it could, conviction settling into place as he let it out. With a gentle motion the door swung open, and there she was.

"Shoshanna."

She tilted her head, ashy hair tumbling over her shoulder as she beheld him. The fire burned low in his belly, muscles frozen as she leant forward in his chair.

"Watterson, good. I've been waiting for you."

"What, waiting to confess?"

"To what?"

The trembling started, teeth grinding together so hard he heard them crack. *To what?* Shoshanna would say Evie's name if he had to pull it from that condescending, vitriol-spilling mouth himself.

"You know what for." The words scraped up his throat, coming out ragged even to himself. It was the apathy that hit hardest, the easy way she stood and blankness of her face. When she sighed he near bit his tongue in half to control his temper.

"You should be thanking me."

"What?"

"How long until you or Cinnabar ended up just like Sevo?"

His heart stopped, breath caught as she gazed at him with knowing blue eyes. She regarded him with the slightest tilt of her head, one that set his teeth on edge.

"You really think she didn't know? Come now, Teach, she's not stupid."

"I don't know what–"

"You haven't forgiven her. And she knows you never will."

"Don't talk about her like that."

"Like what?"

"Like you know her–"

"But I do know her, Teach. Far better than you, apparently."

He held himself back, vibrating with the effort. Ridley's words still bounded about his head: *They deserve more than to be left to bury you.*

Another of Shoshanna's sighs grated against his nerves. "Listen, I could sit here and tell you all about her ideological crises and her grief and regrets but, frankly, I don't want to."

Before he could stop himself, he'd rushed forward, too lost in the mire of his emotions to comprehend the slight smirk on her face. As his fingers closed on her arm a sharp piercing hit his stomach, limbs growing heavy as blood began to dribble around the blade. He watched, paralysed, as Shoshanna's hand twisted it. Pain seared through him as he crumbled, yell tapering off into pained grunts as he pushed his hand against the sluggishly bleeding wound.

"Oh, Watterson, you really need to pay closer attention to your surroundings. How funny." Her grin was sharp as her knife as she looked down at him. "That was always Evie's problem too."

Propelled by her words, he made to stand, an agonising shout tearing from him as she sunk the blade into the back of his knee.

"I've no more time for games, Teach. As much as I'm enjoying this, I've a mind you brought that Shadow with you. She'll have eaten through my fodder by now."

He cringed as the lines of blood made their way down his leg, light-headedness beginning to creep in.

"Then just fucking kill me–"

"Business first. I want the key to Cinnabar's vault."

"You keep away from Modesto."

She looked at him as one would a wayward child, knife still clutched in her bloody hands. "Evie told me about his more ambitious designs. Airships, warships, weapons. I want them."

He coughed a laugh, feeling blood settle on his lips. "What, Shoshanna, you think anyone out there will let the liberationists build themselves a fleet?"

It was her turn to laugh, cutting across him with a sound made up of careless viciousness.

"The liberationists? Please, Teach, some credit. That equality bullshit was Evie's credo, not mine."

"Then what do you want?"

"This." Pain flared through him, a shout tearing past his lips as her fingers dug into the gaping flesh behind his knee. "Carnage is my cause, Teach, and there are plenty out there who'd share in it. They say Myrana's on the brink of a civil war; imagine what the Sidens could do with what your lovely friend can offer."

He was growing colder by the second, blood loss and the icy, clinical tone of her words pushing him further into the dark.

"His family would kill you if you tried."

"What family?"

Oh, Evie. He blinked harshly, head swimming with the need to distract her. "All those people down there, they followed you here. Would die for you…"

"And I'm happy to let them, encourage them, even. You see, it's what I live for, the horror and the spectacle. The cries of the dying, or the anguished weeping of a father over the burnt corpse of his beloved daughter…"

His heart beat heavy in his rattling chest, hate moving thick and sluggish as the sparse blood in his veins.

"Now give me the designs, Teach, or I'll find Cinnabar and play him like a violin. I bet I'll get him to make prettier sounds than you ever could."

Modesto was downstairs, he was so nearby – a Shadow prowling between them wasn't enough. With reluctant, stiff fingers Watt pulled the keys from his pocket, passing the little gold one to her with a snarl.

"If you go near him…"

"Threats at this point will only make you look more pathetic."

He watched as she approached the vault, blinking against the black spots in his visions as she placed the key in the lock. The moment she twisted it, the door exploded off its hinges; her body and debris scattering around his office as he succumbed to the darkness.

He wanted to learn Tegarrat, wanted to roll the words and decipher the curving, beautiful script his nana sent them. His papa always said no, said it was like looking backwards. He'd been born in Gallow just like Watt, and when his parents had moved back to Tegarron he'd not gone with them. His mama was an old-world Galleon, born down in Ocean Heights like the Teaches always had been, moving to Cerrano with power in her veins and a shine to her eyes. His parents had met and been content to have him; Mama didn't give a damn what language he wanted to learn, so long as he learned it well, but still Papa said no.

So when he started school properly, five years old and eager to learn, he could speak Galleon, and only Galleon. But then he'd heard strange sounds, heavy and new; Watt couldn't help but watch the little boy bid farewell to his parents in a strange tongue.

Watt hadn't stopped to think; he'd never been shy and couldn't understand why anyone would be. With quick steps he approached, chubby little face excited and determined.

"Hello."

He had big hazel eyes, this boy, and skin even darker than Watt's. Though Mama had assured him his would get a little darker at least; he sincerely hoped so.

"Hello."

"I'm Watterson Teach. I like being called Watt though."

The boy's grin was big, bright, with shining, wonky teeth prominent in a cheery face. "I'm Ash Marty Sevo. Ash."

"What language were you speaking?"

"When?"

"Before, to your parents."

"Oh, Ajarsi. Don't you speak Ajarsi?"

Watt shook his head – should he speak Ajarsi? Ash sounded surprised he didn't.

"No. I want to speak Tegarrat but my papa won't teach me."

"Why not?"

Watt shrugged; he didn't understand no matter how many times Papa told him.

Ash's eyes brightened; he must have a good idea. "I can teach you Ajarsi if you like?"

Watt's heart leapt. "Really?"

Ash nodded, grabbing his hand; his palms were bigger, but they fit right.

Chapter 32

AFTER THE FIRE

The funeral was such a sombre affair, cloudless blue sky and glaring sun serving as a stark contrast to the mass of grey below. As Lara watched the coffin descend her heart followed suit; it wouldn't be long now. She glanced at Roman, taking in the damaged, baby-pink skin along the right side of that perfect face. It'd scar, they said; the blast had blistered the skin beyond its capability to fully repair, but she was lovely still. Those enchanting eyes found hers, sorrowful against the morning sun. Lara's heart ached; Roman's influence still galloped through her muscles and she couldn't help but wonder how much of a toll it had taken. Did the older woman feel bereft of all that power? Or was she so very strong she'd just that much to spare? Lara didn't know, but as the service droned on, she couldn't turn away.

When the crowd began to shift she moved, sidling and sliding her way to Roman's side, courage caught in her chest.

"Lara?"

"I thought I'd save you the trouble of calling for me later. No point in delaying the inevitable, is there?"

The small, sad smile she received in reply made her ache; gold was proving to be such a kind colour.

"You deserve better than this." Roman glanced over Lara's shoulder, no doubt to the grave of their former leader. "You all do."

"I suppose given the circumstances, you aren't looking for congratulations then, Commissioner Ion?"

"You can call me Roman now, if you'd like."

Something in her lifted suddenly, all that trepidation and imposed regret slipping away under a simple request. "I would. I do."

Roman's eyes were bright, glistening in the sun with pent-up emotion. "I think I'm too young for this, Lara–"

"High Commissioner Ion." Jackie was at the other woman's elbow, tall and sturdy and looking unnervingly calm. "We shouldn't delay, you're still injured and Governor Shine would like a word before we go." She cast a firm gaze at Lara, hand swiftly moving to Roman's shoulder. "Key."

"Jackie."

Those platinum brows arched sharply. "That's Deputy Commissioner King to you, Cadet Key–"

"My name is Lara." As she pulled off her jacket she smiled, a bright, uncontrollable thing that stretched foreign across her cheeks. It was a welcome feeling.

She paused as she turned to go, looking back at Roman with a longing she didn't want to control. Without thinking she moved, arms encircling their young commissioner as softly as they could. Over her shoulder Lara caught Jackie's eye, finding laughter in those orbs to match Roman's against her cheek.

"Thank you." Reluctantly she pulled away, skin still tingling from the contact. "Goodbye, Roman."

With the sun at her back she left the crowd behind, the final notes of the late Commissioner Stone's funeral dying away.

"So our baby commissioner gets a hug and I get fuck all?" Hadren leant against the cemetery gates, looking regal and forthright despite the lazy angle she'd taken. "Where's my fond farewell, Lara?"

"Why would I say goodbye to you when I'll see you tomorrow?" With her jacket still held loose, Lara approached, knocking playfully into Hadren's shoulder.

"Whoa, assaulting an officer already? I can have you detained for that, you know."

"Please, you can't lock me up. I'm wild."

Hadren straightened, tone suddenly serious. "You could have told me what you were doing. I would have helped you."

"I know you would, but I didn't want to ruin this for you. You've worked too hard for it."

"And you haven't?"

"I was worked to it, Hads, it's not the same." It was a relief to watch her friend nod; Hadren always understood. "I'll see you tomorrow. I know your patrols after all."

"Yes, you do. I'm seeing a lot of arrests in our future, Lara."

Lara smirked, backing away playfully. "You'll have to catch me first, Constable Gogh, you and your dog-boy."

Hadren's laughter followed her from the cemetery, ringing in her ears all the way to the Sevo mansion.

Her happy mood stilled as she beheld Andromeda, stood in the grand entrance hall bedecked in the familiar colours of red and silver. Lara floundered, heady smells of heat and sweet peas doing nothing to clear her head.

"What's this?"

"They offered me a position in the syndicate. Security."

"Sec… why? When?"

Red suited Andromeda, clashed wonderfully against the burnt caramel of her skin and the dark of her hair. Lara's eye caught the strip of skin where her silver-lined collar ended and wondered, not for the first time, what she might taste like.

"Yesterday, after Watterson was safe. Modesto asked me."

"What about the Citadel?"

"I'm from Berra, Lara, I follow real power. It's become increasingly clear to me that in this city, it's shifting."

Lara felt very out of place all of a sudden, grey jacket hanging heavy and useless in her hand.

"Did they tell you?"

She blinked, meeting Andromeda's questioning gaze. "Sorry?"

"Ion and King – did they tell you what happened to Shoshanna?"

"Oh, uh, yes. They've sent her to Princetown slightly less than the woman she was."

The other woman snarled, teeth bright between those reddened lips. "It's better than she deserves. That failsafe should have killed her."

“If Ridley hadn’t shown up I’m sure it would have.” Even to her own ears she sounded strained, voice thin and reedy in the grand room. Eventually she managed to choke out, “How’s Teach? Better?”

“Oh yes, driving Modesto to distraction already.”

“Lara, just who I was hoping to see.”

Said girl startled, staring up at Leon with a churning stomach. The older woman descended the stairs with a skip in her step, a smile lessening the sharpness of her features.

“You wanted to see me?”

“Of course. Andromeda tells me you’re no longer a Greycoat.”

Lara’s ears burned, her blush no doubt as red as their uniforms. She would have been annoyed, but Andromeda looked pleased when she glimpsed her, almost as pleased as Leon.

“Not as of today, no.”

“Good, then you must need a job.”

Well, this day was proving to be full of surprises.

Leon’s arm settled warm over her shoulders, leading her deeper into the house. “Walk with me, Lara; I’ve plans that require someone of your talents. You let me know what you think of them.”

Joy bubbled up anew; she’d never been asked that before.

Chapter 33

TAKE CARE

Something about Wes Sevo made her think he'd be useful someday; useful to her. Ridley could keep on the child's good side until then; he was already staring at her like she hung the moons.

"How much?" Although his unblinking gaze was a little unnerving.

"How much what, boy?"

He huffed, fondly of course; everything he did was that way inclined. "How much do I owe you for saving Watt and Mods?" Oh, right – they'd had a deal.

"Nothing, Wes."

"That's not right, though; I asked you to look after them and you did. I have to hold up my end of the bargain."

She sighed, senses overwhelmed by the scent of so many flowers – how did any of them get anything done in this place?

"I would have saved Watt anyway, and as regards Modesto it's not me you should be thanking."

He waved his hand imperiously, puppyish limbs lending the gesture a ridiculous air. "Lara and Andy are taken care of – Leon's hired them."

"I'm not really after a job."

"I know *that*, but I need to give you something."

She laughed as he sulked, dropping sullenly onto Watt's office chair.

"Money?"

"I've got money, Wes."

"Modesto's hand?"

The laugh burst out of her before she could stop it, throat singing and chest heaving with it. It'd been too long since mirth had rattled round her ribcage.

Wes was aghast. "What? He's lovely and smart and can almost cook without setting things on fire. I dare you to do better."

She blinked back tears, still chuckling at the seriousness of his face.

"I'm sure he can, but I doubt he'd appreciate you offering him up like some sort of prize. Besides, I have Friday. And would you really be happy for him to leave? Would Watt?"

"Oh, you're right; he'd be upset if Mods went anywhere." Wes nodded sagely; she'd let him keep his innocence. "I mean, the last time someone tried to talk to Modesto Watt fired them. Then they started arguing in his office and stuff smashed and Dad took me out for a walk." Then again, maybe he'd already lost it.

"Look, Wes, how about you just owe me, all right? I'll collect when I need to."

He chewed on his lip, looking as serious as a twelve-year-old could at a full-sized desk. Eventually he nodded, holding out his hand.

"Deal." His hand was already a little bigger than hers. "They want to speak with you before you leave."

"All right. Nice doing business with you, Wes Sevo."

"Nice doing business with *you*, Ridley Ripley."

She heard them from down the hall, muffled voices increasing in volume as she stood there, silent on the other side of the door. By the Mother, surely they didn't want to thank her again? Reluctantly she knocked, a yelp preceding the call to enter.

When she let herself in she took in the scene with only a raised eyebrow. Watt was sat up in bed, an overly pleased smile on his face and not a hint of his previously ashy pallor in sight. Modesto was stood a foot or so from the bed, shirt half open and rather flushed. He was fiddling conspicuously with his collar, only managing to make it lie less flat.

"Am I interrupting?"

"Yes–"

"No–"

Watt's smile only widened at their answers.

Modesto growled. "No, you're not. Watt's just proving how well you healed him."

"I'm sure he is."

Now that she was close enough Ridley spied slightly darkened patches of skin peeking from beneath Modesto's collar. Well healed indeed.

"Wes said you wanted to talk to me."

"We've just been told Shoshanna's been sent to Princetown, minus an arm and most of a leg. We thought you'd want to know she can't cause you or anyone else trouble any more." Despite the earnestness in Watt's words the cold crept in; guilt no longer willing to be ignored. "There are still some of her people out there, but without her I doubt it'll be much longer till they're rounded up. With any luck, they'll realise that violence hasn't done them any favours."

"And Evie?"

Watt grimaced. "They've had a truth-seeker to see her. Since she's been so cooperative and earnest in her repentance it looks as though she'll only get a minimum sentence. And it'll be here, they won't be shipping her off after Shoshanna."

"That's not so bad, then."

"Um…" Modesto glanced to Watt and then back to Ridley, pulling on his shirtsleeves. "We were wondering if you'd come to her trial. It might… it might help if they see you've forgiven her too. After everything that happened to you." They must have taken her silence for reticence, because he quickly went on. "Sorry, only if you want to. It's a lot to ask."

Ridley smiled at him. "No, no, it's not a lot. Not really."

She left them hastily with a promise to return the next day; apparently dinner was the least they could do after all she'd done for them. The thought of food made her stomach roll.

As she walked through Cerrano she couldn't help but wonder at each person she passed. Did they know? Were they missing someone? Had Ridley obliterated the love of their life in a puddle of blood?

By the time she reached the tower she was shaking, heart jackhammering against her ribs and stomach threating to rebel. She collapsed, heaving to her knees on the dusty floor, the booming crack registering in her ears but not her bones. Back down again – was this how all monsters felt? Her nails splintered upon the floorboards as she dug into them, breaths sputtering as her throat convulsed. The metallic tang of blood was still on her tongue – all that was left of those people.

Warm hands cupped her face, chasing away the cold and tilting her head to meet those stormy grey eyes she knew so well.

"Ridley."

"I… I killed them, Friday. I couldn't control myself – every single one…–" Her throat seized as she choked out the words, wheezing as tears streamed hot down her face.

Friday leant in closer. "I know."

"A-all of them. Till there was… nothing left."

"You did what you had to do."

"I lost control."

Those hands tightened, fingertips digging with bruising force at the back of her neck. The pain pulled her up, lungs and heart finally calming.

"You did what needed to be done."

"They didn't deserve it."

"Perhaps, but it's what they got."

Slowly, Friday's fingers came away, standing with a hand out to Ridley. Shakily she took it, being pulled easily to stand despite the unsteady tremble of her legs.

"Just because I saved Teach and Shoshanna doesn't mean the Greycoats won't come. Someone needs to answer for those deaths."

"After all this time, you think I'd let the Greycoats take you from me? Seven hundred years hasn't taught you a thing, has it?"

"It's taught me some things."

"Like what?"

"Like if you don't want me to go, I won't go."

Friday smiled serenely, leaning down to press a tender kiss on the corner of Ridley's mouth.

"Centuries later and you're still cleaning up my mistakes?"

"Of course, girl, it's the only way I can keep you."